The Past is Present

Kathleen Webb

Clink
Street

London | New York

Published by Clink Street Publishing 2018

Copyright © 2018

First edition.

ISBN:
978-1-912562-01-5 paperback
978-1-912562-02-2 ebook

For Natalie, Miranda, Jackson and Paloma,
Martin and Jon, Louise and Sarah, my wonderful family.

For Linda, Gilly, Chris and Bev., my dear friends.

For Roy – I miss you so much.

All the flowers of all the tomorrows are in the seeds of today.
Chinese proverb

PART ONE

Monday

Chapter 1
2010

It was a day like any other, but Catherine Morgan had little idea how this day would change her life and change it forever...

Monday morning arrived soon enough. She woke early to a gloomy, dull overcast sky which she glimpsed through the opening of the white painted plantation shutters in the window opposite her bed. "So much for the forecast of a warm sunny day; they never seem to get it right, do they?" she muttered to herself, stretching her arm across the small cabinet by the side of the bed to switch off her digital alarm clock. The dial shone bright luminous green and the time showed 6 a.m.

Catherine had allowed herself plenty of time to prepare for her interview at Braeside School, scheduled for 9.30 that morning. She couldn't be late. She'd waited over a year for this opportunity and at last an opening had become available for a teacher with her qualifications. All the paperwork had been forwarded to the school and now the day had finally arrived. A position at this prestigious school would be perfect.

Stepping into her old comfy slippers and pulling her white towelling robe around her, Catherine made her way downstairs for a cup of tea before showering and dressing for the day ahead.

The water in the shower was warm and inviting. She lingered a moment longer than necessary. The perfume from the scented body wash she had purchased at the airport on her return from her backpacking trip to the Far East, left the steam filled bathroom full of the intoxicating aroma of oriental flowers, which seemed to hang delicately in the air.

For the interview she had painstakingly chosen a simple navy blue wool suit, a crisp white cotton blouse and a pair of low-heeled navy blue leather court shoes. She wore a few pieces of silver Jewellery, very little makeup and just a touch of lip gloss to enhance her full lips. Her newly washed hair was tied neatly back in a ponytail.

"If this doesn't impress, then I don't know what will," she said to herself. Catherine had always denied herself the luxury of buying designer clothes. For one, she couldn't afford them and she didn't have the need to buy what she termed as 'overpriced branded items' to feel good. She felt comfortable buying her clothes from the usual high-street chain stores and lounging about in a pair of old jeans and an oversized jumper.

"I think my qualifications are pretty good. I worked hard to achieve them, let's hope they are good enough for Braeside School. Well I will know soon enough," she sighed.

Modest by nature with a somewhat fiery disposition, Catherine Morgan, a strikingly attractive 24-year-old young woman, stood five feet seven inches tall. She had little idea just how attractive she was. This feature of her personality was quite endearing and compliments to this effect were frequent. Her skin was fair, and porcelain in its appearance, and was only slightly overshadowed by her long dark hair. Her eyes, which looked in daylight to be a soft velvet brown colour, sometimes appeared a shade darker because of her thick dark lashes.

***

It seemed like a lifetime ago, but just three months had passed since Catherine moved away from her family home in Cambridgeshire, England, the house she had shared with her parents Greg and Valerie Morgan for the best part of her life. Her parents had died in a tragic road accident three years earlier leaving her alone in the large family house.

The move from the family home in Cambridgeshire had been no easy task for Catherine. There had been many boxes and belongings of her parents to sort through. Items she could never think of getting rid of. Items not just of monetary value, but of sentimental value too, these she packed and took with her to her new home. The rest she gave to various charities in her local high street.

Catherine's new home was now a quaint slate-fronted cottage in a small picturesque fishing village called Port Isaac. Situated on the north side of Cornwall just south of Tintagel, Port Isaac boasted a famous stream that ran through the village finding its way into the sea over the harbour wall. There was also an abundance of narrow winding streets, many lined with old white-washed cottages, which gave shelter to local fishermen and their families working in the area.

The cottage was in need of a lot of TLC when Catherine purchased it. But nevertheless it was a bargain which was reflected in the price she paid. Knowing it was a huge project to undertake and it would take her a long time to finish, she was all the more determined to do most of the work herself, and decided she would only employ outside workers for the really big jobs beyond her skills.

The view from the front of the cottage was worth all the extra work she would have to do inside the house. Stepping out of the front door, you couldn't help but marvel at the scene across the bay. A stunning vista as far as the eye could see, and the sea air, clear and fresh.

***

Around six months ago Catherine had begun to suffer from the occasional headache. Steadily they increased over a short period of time. She'd been to see her doctor and visited two different hospitals, with appointments for various scans and tests, but nothing had shown. In the last month, thankfully the headaches had ceased, only to be replaced by a more serious and sinister symptom which led to Catherine finding herself in a very dark place. Her spirits dulled, her enthusiasm gone, and her mind playing tricks on her, she began gradually to experience strange dreams and day-time visions. They would appear at the most inopportune moments. She never knew when or where they would occur and inevitably they had become more disturbing. It was if someone was trying to tell her something. What was it Catherine was seeing in her dreams that seemed unfamiliar, yet compelling enough to show her that these visions in some way were connected to her? "But how," Catherine questioned.

Catherine decided to see her own Doctor – Doctor Travers once more. She hoped he would perhaps prescribe something to help her sleep and get some much needed rest. She didn't want the dreams to stop altogether, as she wanted to find out exactly what they were trying to tell her, if anything. But she needed to sleep now, if only to get on with her life.

Doctor Travers, an experienced and distinguished middle-aged man, took his time chatting to her, taking up most of her full ten minute appointment. After thoroughly examining and questioning Catherine, he passed her a hand written prescription for a short course of anti-depressant tablets. "Try these Catherine. They should help you sleep and lessen your anxiety." He also advised her to come back to see him in a couple of weeks to see how she was getting on. Willing to try anything, Catherine readily agreed. "Maybe these pills will give me some form of escape for a while," she muttered to herself as she unscrewed the brown safety bottle, popped a pill in her mouth and swallowed it with a sip of still water from a small bottle she kept in the fridge. Unsure of what was happening to her, she was now even more determined to get to the bottom of it.

Catherine had only confided up to now in her best friend Miranda. However she had a feeling there was only one person who could really help her, and that was her Aunt Izzy. Now that her parents were gone, she had no other living relatives that she knew of. Aunt Izzy wasn't a blood relative, but she could just as well have been. Catherine was extremely fond of her aunt and they were very close. "I think something in my past may be the key to unlocking the reason for the dreams and anxiety attacks I'm having. I've got a strange suspicion that Aunt Izzy could have the answer," Catherine debated to herself. But what could Aunt Izzy possibly know, Catherine puzzled...

***

The weather outside began to brighten. The clouds had dispersed leaving in their wake a bright and vivid blue sky and a warm sea breeze.

Catherine took her car keys from the glass table in the hall. Gathering her bag from the small occasional chair next to the table, she walked out of the front door, locking the door behind her, and headed towards her car and the short journey to Braeside School...

Chapter 2
2010

It was a bright sunny day, perfect in every way, except for a slight chill that could be felt in the early morning breeze. The pale azul sky portrayed not a cloud and the drive down the narrow leafy lane was every inch a picture postcard. Catherine glanced at the fields either side of her as she drove several miles further on. On the left-hand side of the lane, corn could be seen growing in abundance as far as the eye could see. On the right-hand side, rape covered the whole field like a blanket of yellow flowers, contrasting well with the occasional red of the poppy flower, protruding intermittently amongst the hedgerow of wild grasses lining the edge of the lane.

Catherine continued on down the lane, listening to the annoying American accent of the woman talking to her on her satellite navigation system until she finally announced; "you have now arrived at your destination."

"At last," Catherine thought to herself. It was further than she had originally anticipated. She was glad now that she had left a little earlier than she needed to. On the approach to the entrance of the school grounds she saw a long curving driveway outstretched in front of her. She could just make out that it terminated right in front of a rather grand impressive looking house. Catherine might have been forgiven for thinking that the old grand house (now Braeside School) had 'jumped' straight out of a Dickens' novel but for the modern touches of a well-designed car park, displaying personalised name plaques for each of the individual members of staff. The newly laid block paving finishing at the entrance of the school, was another give away. You knew then that you were in the 21st Century.

Just several metres from the front door to the school stood a large raised circular flower bed, displaying a magnificent array of colourful 'busy lizzies and 'alyssum' flowers, adding much needed colour to the rather old and drab appearance of the building.

Catherine drove cautiously into the car park. She quickly found a space with no visible name plate, parked her car, stretched her arm behind her and took her leather handbag from the rear seat. She felt around inside the bag and found her hairbrush. Pulling the rear-view mirror towards her, she brushed her hair and turned off the car's engine. Stepping out of the car, and fumbling with the large bunch of keys that were never out of her possession, she eventually located the car's fob and pressed the top button to lock her old white Mini Cooper. Walking hastily, Catherine made her way out from the car park up to the large entrance door.

Originally a grand stately home, Braeside House had been converted in recent years to a boarding school. The facia of the house was prominently stone, and Catherine thought in all probability it must have dated back to the late 1700s. A magnificent wooden door took centre stage. It was painted black with a high gloss finish. The brass door furniture consisted of an ornate circular knocker, placed strategically at eye level. The intricate large hinges each side of the entrance door were highly polished, and gleamed splendidly in the early morning sunshine.

Catherine lifted the brass knocker and knocked several times. The sound seemed to resonate throughout the entire building. Almost immediately the door creaked open.

"Good morning. Can I help you?" asked the mature and surly looking woman, ushering Catherine into the lobby. "Yes, thank you. I'm here for an interview with the Head Master – Mr Castona – at 9.30." "And your name?" the woman asked. "My name is Catherine Morgan," Catherine replied nervously. "Please take a seat. Someone will be along directly."

Catherine sat down in the lobby on a rather old and a little shabby, antique armchair. It was upholstered in a red and gold damask fabric; it was entirely comfortable and sat well in its grand surroundings.

Catherine didn't have to wait long. She could hear the faint sound of approaching footsteps getting closer as a young lady walked into the lobby. "Catherine Morgan," she announced. "Please follow me."

Catherine promptly rose from the chair, her belongings in hand. She walked quickly, following closely behind the woman who was much younger than the lady who had greeted her on her arrival. This young woman was not unattractive by any means. She was slim with short wavy hair that she tucked neatly behind her ears but which unfortunately revealed a small unsightly scar on one side of her face, about an inch in length. This left Catherine wondering what had caused her injury. Her legs were sturdy, and on her feet she wore old-fashioned sensible brown brogue shoes. She walked with a slight limp, but manoeuvred well along the corridor until she approached a large office at the end of the hallway. There was something about her that didn't quite sit happily with Catherine. She couldn't put her finger on it, but she could, to all intents and purposes, be an attractive woman. So, why would she dress beyond her years? Before Catherine had a chance to gather her thoughts she was ushered into the large office. The Head Master, Martin Castona, sat waiting for her.

"Hello Catherine, I'm very pleased to meet you, my name is Martin Castona. I'm the Headmaster of Braeside School. Please take a seat. Did you bring your CV with you?"

"Yes I have it here." Catherine took the CV out from her handbag and handed it across the desk to the Headmaster.

"Well Catherine, your qualifications are exemplary, and I see you have recently taken a teacher training course in London, for which you achieved very good results indeed."

"Yes. Thank you, sir," Catherine replied. "Earlier this year I travelled quite a bit, backpacking in Asia and Africa, and on my return six months ago, I decided at that point to pursue a career in teaching. After visiting several schools in the poorer areas of South Africa, mainly the Eastern Cape, you would be hard of character, if you weren't extremely moved on seeing the poverty and lack of education that these children have to endure daily. I had thought, at one point, of staying in South Africa, to teach in one of the 'disadvantaged areas', but unfortunately, as I lost my parents several years ago, I knew I had to return home to sort things out, and make a life for myself here in England.

"After much deliberating, and a little help from my best friend, I decided to 'up sticks' and move house. I have always loved the Cornish coast, and the fact that my friend also lived here helped make my decision that Cornwall was to be my new home, and once settled, I could seriously look for an opening in a nearby school.

"I noticed your advert in the local *Gazette*, and thought this could be just the position I was looking for. I had very little idea the school would be such a grand and beautiful old house – so much history, I think?"

"Yes," the Headmaster replied, we certainly have our share of that."

Martin Castona continued glancing over Catherine's CV making written notes, highlighting certain paragraphs and asking additional questions. As he did so, he took off his black rimmed spectacles and placed them on the green, leather-covered desk top in front of him, before turning to Catherine and asking; "Miss Morgan, if you were to be offered the post of junior teacher, it would entail you teaching English and History to a class of nine-year-old boys, and taking the occasional Physical Education class – perhaps twice a week for a short while. I see from your CV you have a degree in English, History and Geography, therefore you are qualified for the post, but without a qualification in Physical Education. However, I do not think that this would necessarily be a problem. The Physical Education classes would only be short term until we find a replacement for Mr Grant, who is retiring at the end of this term. I am sure you could manage twenty, nine-year-old energetic boys for half an hour, once or twice a week?" The Headmaster smiled at Catherine, as they both quietly laughed.

"I so want this job," Catherine thought to herself. She sat waiting patiently for Mr Castona to make several more written notes on her CV.

The Head Master continued interviewing Catherine. After an exhausting ten minutes or so of interaction, he had made a decision. "Well, Miss Morgan, it's not usual for me to offer a post as junior teacher at this school without a second interview. I have had several other applicants, all quite highly qualified and with some experience, but I do feel confident, even at this stage of the proceedings, and in view of your lengthy interview today, that I would like to offer you the post of junior teacher here at Braeside School".

"There will be the usual trial of three months settling in period, to see if you like it here, and if things work out mutually for both parties, we can then welcome you officially as a permanent member of staff."

"You're starting salary we have already discussed and other incidentals, including health care, pension, holidays etc., we can discuss at a later date, if these terms are acceptable to you."

"Are there any questions you would like to ask me? If not, what do you say Catherine?" ...

Chapter 3
2010

Catherine sat in front of the Headmaster for what seemed an eternity before she spoke. Not because she was unsure of her answer, but because she didn't want to seem too eager to accept straight away, the job offered to her. Clearing her throat, Catherine replied...

"Mr Castona, I would be very happy to accept your offer, and could start next week if that's OK with you?" Catherine coughed trying hard to hide her excitement. The Headmaster replied; "Good, that's settled then Catherine." I'm glad you have accepted the post and I look forward to seeing you next Monday at 8.30, you will then be introduced to form 8B, the class you will be teaching this year."

The woman who had previously showed Catherine into the Headmaster's study, appeared at the door. "Miss Galloway will take you to the Secretary's office just to fill in a few details that we require, and you can be on your way, as I'm sure you have a lot to do before next Monday." Martin Castona stood from his desk, shook Catherine's hand and said goodbye.

"Oh, just one other matter Catherine. We do require appropriate clothing – so no miniskirts please, but I'm sure this won't be a problem for you. I look forward to seeing you Monday then," and gestured a wave goodbye.

When Catherine had left the Headmaster's study, Martin Castona immediately picked up the phone. He dialled a long distance number to the USA.

"Hello, can I help you?" snapped the sharp muffled voice on the end of the line.

"Hi, it's Martin. We've got Catherine Morgan. She's accepted the post. She's starting next Monday the 8th, so I'll be able to keep a close watch on her."

"That's good news Martin. Please let me know immediately if there are any further developments," the voice replied with relief.

"I will, sir, goodbye." Martin replaced the receiver.

Catherine followed Miss Galloway down the corridor. She passed various classrooms, where most of the pupils seemed to be deep in concentration in their lessons, and many raising their hands eagerly, in answer to a question put by their teacher. She noticed a variety of pictures on the walls of the corridor, painted by pupils of the school – some very good – others perhaps needing a little work, but none-the-less, good efforts by these children, some aged as young as five years old.

"Here we are," said Miss Galloway, "the secretary Mrs Palmer will take all the necessary details from you, it won't take too long. Would you like a cup of tea or coffee?" "Yes that would be nice. Tea please," Catherine replied with a certain amount of relief. "How do you take your tea Miss Morgan?" "Milk no sugar, thank you," Catherine replied.

Catherine sat down and proceeded to answer the questions put to her by the secretary. The school secretary, Mrs Palmer, a middle-aged lady of rather large proportions, had a serious face. Her reading glasses rested precariously on the end of her nose, which gave the impression of her being officious and unapproachable. But Catherine found her to be warm and welcoming.

Miss Galloway handed Catherine her tea in a bone china tea cup and saucer. The red rose design on the cup was slightly faded with time, but beautiful none the less, and was not unlike that of her Aunt Isabelle's Royal Albert tea set in America. Miss Galloway also offered Catherine a selection of shortbread biscuits placed on a small silver tray. "How grand, I think I am going to like it here at Braeside School," Catherine smiled to herself.

When all questions had been fully answered, Catherine thanked Mrs Palmer and made her way out of the school. When she reached the front door and stepped out into the warm midday sunshine, she stopped and looked across the fields towards the sea. "I'm sure I am going to be very happy here," she thought to herself.

Catherine walked the short distance to the car park. She got into her car and before she could turn the ignition on, her mobile phone rang. – "Hi Miranda" – Catherine answered – "how are you?"

"I'm fine Catherine, more to the point, how did you get on with your interview this morning?"

"I got the job Miranda, yes I actually got it! Can you believe it?" Catherine replied excitedly.

"Look I've got a few hours to spare before picking the kids up from school, how about going for a coffee at the new coffee shop in the harbour, and you can tell all?" Miranda asked.

"That sounds great, see you there in 15 minutes," Catherine confirmed. She turned on the ignition of her car, put her mobile phone back in her bag, placed the bag on the passenger seat, and set off for the harbour.

Catherine arrived ten minutes later at the coffee shop. She found that Miranda was already seated at the table that looked out over the harbour, waiting for her. The café was beautifully decorated in cream and black with beach wood tables. Most tables were covered with a white starched tablecloth and in the centre of each table a small bud vase was placed containing a single yellow rose.

Miranda had already ordered two cappuccinos and two lemon muffins, knowing full well how much Catherine loved lemon muffins.

Their coffees and muffins arrive and they thank the waitress.

"Well Catherine, tell me what happened at the interview," Miranda asked eagerly.

"The Headmaster was very nice. It was a long interview, but I was offered the job without a second interview, a bit unusual I thought, and he offered me the job there and then. I can't believe how lucky I am," Catherine spoke slightly bemused. "Not to worry, I've got the job and that is all that matters, eh Miranda?"

"That is a bit unusual," Miranda confirmed, "but the Headmaster must have been very impressed with you Catherine."

"His name is Martin Castona. He's about 40, quite good looking – dark blond hair, lovely smile – but too old for me, Miranda, just in case you've got any ideas," Catherine replied. They both laughed at the thought.

"I start next Monday, with a class of nine-year-olds, so I have a lot of preparation to do, but I'm not sure yet how the school is run, so I'll ease myself into it slowly," Catherine confirmed.

"You'll be fine, I know you Catherine Morgan," said Miranda. "Miss Efficient! Have you had any more flashbacks or headaches recently? You know you see things others don't Catherine. I always thought you were a bit spooky!!" Miranda said, smiling sympathetically.

"Yes I seem to be desiderating more and more. I am a bit worried, the last flashback I experienced was in an area I didn't recognise, very open and surrounded by grass. There was a large building nearby – it looked like a school. I was watching a soccer match – so much razzmatazz. There were school cheerers with colourful outfits, waiving their pom-poms. The stadium was packed. I recall there was a spectator's scoreboard, but I don't know where it was or who was there. I wish I could remember more," Catherine replied.

"I'm sure in time you will Catherine, don't stress too much. Try and write down what you remember and where it might be, and maybe in time we can unravel this mystery," Miranda comforted Catherine.

Catherine and Miranda finished their coffee in thoughtful silence. They said their goodbyes and promised to meet up again, the following week...

Chapter 4
24 Years Earlier

Life couldn't have been any more fulfilling for Rachael and Susie. A life in the USA in late 1985 was good for both girls. Growing up together in the same neighbourhood (with its tree-lined avenues and mixture of quaint and diverse shops) ensured they saw a lot of each other over the years. They were pretty much inseparable.

Susie was a wild child, an outgoing free spirit. Her wavy hair was a beautiful shade of auburn. It hung freely down her back to her waist. She had a pale complexion, paired with agreeable features and a plethora of freckles that spread across her nose. It made her all the more attractive. Her mother always said she was born too late. She almost probably would have been very happy as a 'hippy' living in the peaceful era of the psychedelic flower power period of the early 70s.

Rachael was the more grounded of the two. Sensible, not a risk taker like her friend, which helped on more than one occasion to keep Susie's feet firmly on the ground. That was no mean feat. Rachael was the taller of the two. Her hair was long, straight and very dark, almost black; combined with her olive complexion, it made the perfect combination, complimenting her sultry brown eyes. She had a near perfect hourglass figure that was the envy of many of her friends. Both girls were quite stunning in their respective ways.

Rachael and Susie were born in the wealthy suburb of New Haven. It was one of those places large enough to be interesting yet small enough to be friendly. Living only a short distance from Yale, it was pure luck that both were accepted to the same college. They had worked so hard, revising continually most evenings, well into the early hours of the morning to achieve their above average grades.

Rachael was awarded a tennis scholarship to Yale for her skills on the court. She was an exceptional and talented tennis player, and full of hope, like many others before her, of perhaps one day becoming a professional player. She realised there would be endless hours of back-breaking hard work ahead if she was to reach the heady heights of the US Open or Wimbledon, her dream, and she felt lucky that both her parents were completely committed to her succeeding, and would support her in every way possible. Lowering her sights slightly, there was always the Yale Bulldogs to aspire to.

"What do you think the odds were of us both being accepted to Yale?" Susie asked excitedly.

"Probably about 1,000 to 1 but stranger things have happened," Rachael laughed "and I think my parents are more excited than I am. We should start looking for part-time work to help with the additional costs. There won't be an awful lot more opportunities before we start college, and I don't think it will be easy, there will be hundreds of students looking for work," Rachael insisted.

"Mmmm... I suppose you're right," Susie replied, knowing full well she would rather visit the local shopping centre than wait on tables in Denny's. "But needs must," she thought to herself, and she went along with the idea, if only to appease Rachael.

The next day both girls rose early. Rachael left home at 8 a.m. and drove to Susie's house. The early morning sun could be seen peeping gently through the leaves on the trees as she drove steadily down the suburban street to where Susie lived. Rachael's car was an old CJ-7 Jeep, a deep turquoise colour with the added luxury of high back leather bucket seats. Although it was over ten years old now and little rusty in parts, it had never let her down, for which she was eternally grateful. Pulling up outside Susie's home and drawing slowly into the curb, Rachael could see Susie sitting on the swing seat on the veranda, waiting patiently for her. Susie could be described as rather scatty by nature, but if there was one aspect of her personality that was an asset to her, it was her punctuality. She was never late.

Rachael hooted her horn. There was no need. She could see Susie waving frantically to her from the veranda. Taking her white leather shoulder bag off the wooden seat, Susie ran down the veranda steps, onto the front lawn and jumped into Rachael's car.

It was an especially pleasant sunny day. The girls drove down the tree lined avenue and headed to the shops on Chapel Street. The early morning sun shone down brightly on the windscreen of Rachael's car, making it all the more difficult to navigate the road easily. Nevertheless, they arrived safely, parked the car in the nearest parking lot and walked the short distance to the main shopping centre.

It was now 8.45 a.m. Chapel Street was relatively empty of shoppers, save a few shop assistants on their way to work. "Let's go to Denny's for breakfast," Susie suggested. "The shops don't open for at least another half hour. We're too early and I am starving. I didn't have time for breakfast before we left." Rachael hadn't had breakfast either so readily agreed. They headed to Denny's for blueberry pancakes and coffee.

Susie was far more concerned about buying her dress for the graduation prom than looking for part-time work. "Rachael, I'd like to have a quick look for a prom dress before we start hunting for work. We've got plenty of time, all day in fact, and I've seen a chiffon dress in a boutique just a little further up Chapel Street. It's to die for!!" she implored.

"This is madness Susie. We came here to look for work, not to buy a prom dress!!" Rachael replied, rather annoyed.

"I know, but it won't take long. Please Rachael," Susie pleaded, knowing full well Rachael would probably agree after a short exchange of words. "OK, OK, you have fifteen minutes, that's all, and then we start looking for work," Rachael insisted.

They quickly finished their breakfast, paid the bill and made their way back to Chapel Street. An array of assorted boutiques, bistros and individual shops came into view as they turned the corner and walked to the end of the street. "This is it," Susie exclaimed, walking at a much quicker pace to reach the boutique with the pink chiffon dress on a mannequin prominently positioned right in the centre of the window.

The boutique window showed various full-sized mannequins. On them, the window dresser had cleverly displayed mostly prom dresses of various designs and colours, knowing full well the current teenage need for their yearly Prom Ball. "It's that time of year again," Susie thought to herself, peering through the shop window and into the store. The small boutique was full of teenage girls and their mothers who had previously made appointments for their daughters to come and try on their dresses.

"Good morning madam. Can I help you?" the shop assistant asked in a soft voice. "Well yes, could you tell me how much the dark pink chiffon dress in the window is please?" Susie replied, hoping that it wouldn't be too expensive, but secretly knowing that it probably was. Susie's parents had agreed to buy her a prom dress but they were not as well off financially as Rachael's parents and if the dress was expensive, she knew she wouldn't have a chance in hell of her parents agreeing to buy it for her.

"One moment please and I will check for you," the shop assistant replied, as she made her way over to the window display.

She returned moments later with the pink chiffon dress delicately draped over her arm. "This dress is $199.95. Would you like to try it on? We have one booth free at the moment," the shop assistant insisted, pointing to the open booth. As Susie had feared, it was far too expensive. She felt her face turning a bright shade of crimson before replying. "Ah! Okay thank you for your help. I'll think about it," and she turned slowly but exited promptly out of the boutique, followed closely by Rachael.

"Well?" Rachael exclaimed. "Are you going to try it on or not?"

"I don't know, I think mum might freak out. It's a bit expensive, isn't it?"

"Look, you really want the dress don't you?" Rachael said sympathetically. "Go and try it on, just to see how it looks. If you like it, you can tell your mum, and then you can come back with her and discuss how to pay for it! Maybe you can help pay towards it from your savings." Several moments passed before both girls walk sheepishly back into the boutique.

"Well, hello again, did you want to try the pink dress on now madam?" the shop assistant asked curtly. "Yes please, size six," Susie replied.

"Very well," please wait here and I'll get the dress for you. Size six you say," as she lowered her spectacles and looked Susie slowly up and down. "Yes size six," Susie said again.

"I don't think she believes I'm a size six. Let's hope it fits, eh Rachael?" Susie said, quietly stifling a giggle.

Rachael and Susie wait for several moments before the shop assistant returned with the dress for Susie to try on. "You can use this changing room here if you wish," said the shop assistant, handing the dress gently to Susie. "Ok thank you." Susie took the prom dress from the assistant and entered the small cubicle. The chrome rings on the top of the curtain clanged together noisily when she drew the heavy curtain behind her. Placing the dress on the small purple velvet chair in the corner of the dressing room, she undressed quickly, and slipped carefully into the chiffon dress.

A short time passed. Susie drew the curtain aside once more, and walked out of the dressing room...

"Wow!!! It looks stunning Susie, and it fits perfectly," Rachael declared.

The prom dress that Susie had chosen was a mid-length style dress. It had a cummerbund of pale pink chiffon draped in folds softly around the waist. Sewn onto the band were crystals and beads that sparkled effortlessly as they reflected the light. The bodice was strapless and tight fitting, in a darker shade of pink, to match the full and flowing skirt, with numerous tiny fabric-covered buttons that fastened down the back of the bodice to the waist.

"Well? Do you like it Rachael?" Susie asked. Rachael hesitated slightly before answering. She knew the dress Susie had chosen was a far cry from something she would have chosen for herself. Does she tell Susie what she really thought of the dress, and that it was a little garish? Or lie?

"It's beautiful Susie, and you look good. You must tell your mum and bring her down to see it." Rachael decided to be economic with the truth on this occasion.

Susie's face was a picture of happiness as she returned to the cubicle. Slipping out of the prom dress as quickly as possible, whilst trying not to damage the fabric, she changed back into her own clothes and drew back the cubicle curtain.

"Is the dress suitable for you?" the shop assistant asked. "Yes, it's perfect, but I will have to return with my mother and try it on once more," Susie replied, handing the dress very gently back to the shop assistant. "Very well, please tell your mother to make an appointment as we are extremely busy right now, as you can see."

Susie and Rachael glanced at each other, both trying to keep a straight face. "Gosh she's happy in her work," Susie said sarcastically. "I just hope I'm not unlucky enough to see her when I come back with Mum." Laughing, both girls make their way out of the boutique closing the door softly behind them.

"Right Susie, you have had more than your fifteen minutes," Rachael declared, "and now it's time to find work before all the jobs are taken."

"OK," Susie reluctantly agreed. "But later let's take in a movie. *Legend* is showing at the Odeon Cinema. There's this new guy starring in the film. I've not seen him before, his name is Tom Cruise. He's so hot!"

Chapter 5
24 Years Earlier

The graduation prom Susie and Rachael had waited all year for had finally arrived. Susie managed to persuade her mother to let her have the pink chiffon dress she had tried on the previous week. The dress had cost $199.95. "A lot of money for a dress you will probably never wear again," her mother said, knowing full well that she would not see the $50 Susie had promised to put towards the dress from her savings. Susie did feel a little guilty – but not for long. She loved the dress and couldn't wait to wear it.

Rachael had already bought her dress for the Prom Ball the year before when holidaying with her parents in Spain. She found an exclusive but small boutique tucked away in one of the cobbled streets that surrounded the old town of Malaga. In the same narrow street, looking upwards, you could see the tiny balconies protruding from the apartments above. Their intricate wrought-iron work allowed a display of coloured bougainvillea to trail over and around them, scattering petals to the ground, irrespective of the shoppers passing by.

The dress Rachael had chosen was simplicity itself. Plain but fashionable, a halter neck design, in a deep mauve silk fabric, full length and edged with a delicate pink beading. The dress was expensive, but unlike Susie, Rachael had no problem convincing her parents to buy it for her. After all they were substantially well off and would not readily miss the sum of $600 for the dress, matching bag and shoes that Rachael had purchased.

***

Janet and Mike Kruger, Susie's mother and father, often had difficulty making ends meet. Their combined salary just about met the demands of the household bills and left little for luxuries. Mike worked for a local car dealership. He held the position of a senior salesman, and had won several awards for 'best salesperson' of 1984 and 1985. His job sounded rather grand but the salary was not. He was a good man, and worked hard holding down a second job as a security guard at the local museum, two nights a week. This helped a little with their struggling finances.

On the other hand, Janet was an ambitious woman. She was determined, at all costs, to 'keep up with her neighbours'. She worked hard to give her family the best, and placed them in debt on more than one occasion in the pursuit of bettering her family's standing. This caused frequent friction in the Kruger household.

Janet Kruger was employed as a secretary at the local River Valley High School. She had worked there for almost ten years. All three of her children and Rachael attended the school at some stage during the last ten years, so she was able to keep a close eye on them all.

Susie's younger brother Travis was a bright and intelligent boy, similar to Susie, sporty to the extreme, making the soccer, basketball and athletic teams, and was expected to do well. He was a good looking boy. With his blond hair, blue eyes, athletic build and height of 6'2," he was the typical all American boy of his generation, and was particularly popular with the girls.

Sarah, Susie's older sister, was already in her second year of college in Washington, studying journalism and forensics. She looked a lot like Susie. The resemblance was undeniable. She had the same auburn hair, green eyes, pleasant smile and a slim figure. But that's where the similarity ended. Her personality could only be described as 'determined'. She was completely focused, driven and knew exactly what she wanted out of life. Just like her mother.

Susie was awarded a full scholarship, in English and Languages, but nothing less was expected of her. Yale University had been more than pleased to accept her with these qualifications. She too was excited about starting in the new semester.

***

The day of the Prom Ball finally arrived. Both girls were excited, having had their nails and hair done at the beautician's in town. Rachael's father agreed to take them to the Prom as long as they would be ready to leave the ball by midnight.

Rachael and her father left the house at 6.30 pm to collect Susie on the way to the Prom. The car pulled up outside Susie's home where she was waiting, sitting on a swing chair on the porch, looking every inch the beauty queen she could well have been.

Rachael's father drove into the school grounds. Crowds of teenagers could be seen slowly starting to arrive in their chauffeur driven cars. Milling about and chatting and laughing, they began to make their way, into the ball. Susie and Rachael said their goodbyes to Rachael's father and made their way quickly and excitedly towards the entrance of the heavily decorated hall. Standing in the queue with the crowds of teenagers who had been waiting patiently, they eventually passed through the heavy wooden doors and into the hall. Most teenagers were unanimous in their choice of gowns. They were excitable and apprehensive at the same time, but hoping to find a little romance, if only for the summer.

Susie and Rachael had a great time at the Prom. They were both asked by admirers for endless dances during the course of the evening, and numerous non-alcoholic cocktails were consumed. They had each met someone they were strongly attracted to and promised to meet up with them again during the summer break. They exchanged phone numbers, said their goodbyes, and left the Prom just after midnight. Laughing and chuckling at the not so successful dances they had endured during the evening, they made their way over to where Rachael's father had parked his car and was waiting patiently to drive them home...

Chapter 6
2010

Driving back from the Harbour Café and her earlier meeting with Miranda, Catherine arrived home and pulled into her driveway. She made sure her handbrake was securely in place because of the steep incline to the front of her house and the thought of her Mini cascading down the hill, always sent shivers down her spine. Locking the car door, she climbed the steps leading to her front door. The sound of the phone ringing jolted her into action. She quickly unlocked the front door, dropped her bag in the hallway and managed to reach the phone just seconds before the answer phone took over.

"364295," Catherine answered, slightly out of breath. "Hello dear," Aunt Izabelle replied. "How are you? I was so worried when you left to return home to England from your last stay. All those documents and papers that I should have locked away safely, and I didn't, I don't know what I was thinking. I am so sorry Catherine. But perhaps it's for the best now. There is so much that you need to know, and I think the time is right for me to tell you the truth, but not on the telephone," Aunt Izabelle half whispered.

"I am going to book a flight to England in three weeks' time," she continued. "Can I stay with you? I'm so looking forward to seeing you and your new home dear."

"Yes, of course you can. I'll pick you up from the airport when you arrive. I have a job now Aunt Izabelle, teaching in a Public School. The school is a large converted stately home. It's quite imposing and rather grand, and sits in a beautiful spot with views overlooking the sea. I am getting a bit nervous, as I start next week."

"That's understandable dear, your first job, but perfectly wonderful for you, so we have a lot of catching up to do, don't we? I will call you next week with my onward flight details from Heathrow to Cornwall. I do hope that there are no delays. At my age it could be a little stressful, too many complications and I worry Catherine, but it is very important that I see you, so I must come." With that she said "goodbye" and hung up.

***

Catherine's Great Aunt Izabelle, an American national living in the USA and a slightly eccentric eighty-three-year-old, was still working two days a week in a local bookstore. She managed to pedal to work each day on her old reliable red bicycle that she kept padlocked to the back porch veranda of her home. As far as Catherine could ascertain, Izabelle was in good health for an eighty-three-year old lady. The only medical problem she was aware of was her failing eyesight. This problem she knew Izabelle liked to keep safely to herself. She also owned an old 1990 cream VW Beetle car. This was stored away in her garage which was attached to the side of the house, similar to many of the 1970s built properties of that type in the area. The garage still had its original brown wooden panelled door, but was now in desperate need of a coat of paint. Above the main body of the door were four small square windows, letting in just enough natural light to enable you to see once inside.

The VW car had been garaged there as far back as Catherine could remember. But there used to be another car stored in the garage. This car belonged to Teddy, Izabelle's late husband and Catherine assumed that they only used Teddy's car for long journeys and it had been sold long ago.

The Volkswagen Beetle seemed in surprisingly good condition except for a few minor scratches to a bumper which had appeared recently, when Aunt Izabelle miscalculated the distance she allowed between the rear bumper of her car and a concrete post!

Five years had passed and Izzy, as Catherine fondly called her, still missed Teddy terribly. Her marriage had been a happy one, and it stayed that way for almost fifty-eight years. She often said to Catherine, "Don't ask me the secret of a long marriage dear, I don't really know but I think you have to be in tune with each other, enjoy the same things, and there has to be a little 'give and take', it was mostly give on my part," and she laughed at the suggestion, "but it was good for us." Izzy and Teddy were completely devoted to each other and they worked together right up until his death from a sudden heart attack. Izzy never spoke of his death for over a year. She couldn't bring herself to speak his name.

"God, I hope one day, I can find someone special like Teddy, and am half as happy as they were," Catherine smiled to herself.

She never did find out exactly what Izzy and Teddy did for a living, but they were very rarely at home, and travelled a great deal, mostly abroad. Catherine made a mental note to ask Izzy exactly what their line of work was the next time she visited.

There were many holidays that Catherine remembered spending at Izzy's lakeside home. The house was not over large, but homely, she recalled. It had a grey and white painted veranda, with steps leading up to the heavily varnished front door, and a small oval window set above the chrome knocker. If she remembered correctly there was a white slatted wooden swing chair positioned on the left hand side of the veranda. Many an evening was spent there with Izzy, sipping a cool glass of Sauvignon Blanc until the sun eventually disappeared out of sight, leaving behind a bright moon and silence, only to be interrupted by the continual sound of crickets on the front lawn. The colourful wind chimes that hung below the rafters could be seen spiralling down, reflecting the moon's glow. They had been there since Catherine was a child and the sound they made tinkling in the breeze had stayed in her memory over the years. "Happy days," Catherine recalled.

If only she could just have remembered more clearly, that last weekend spent with Izzy. Catherine had taken out an old wooden box she had found in Izzy's kitchen cupboard. It had ornate brass hinges placed on all four corners and inside the box were a great many old family photographs, some sepia in colour that were probably taken before she was born. Catherine wished she had paid more attention at the time. There was a small pile of documents and a birth certificate in the box. She couldn't recall the origin of the birth certificate, but something told her it may well have been hers...

***

Time seemed to pass slowly as Catherine prepared for the following Monday. It was now Saturday midday. She left the house and drove her car down the winding cobbled streets, to the main road and the local delicatessen. The store was 'stocked to the brim'. The homemade produce set under the glass domes, was tempting. There were Cornish pasties and decorated pies, and a selection of iced cupcakes and a large gateau. After finally making her choice, Catherine paid for her groceries, and treated herself to a selection of cupcakes, which the assistant handed to her in a small white box, tied neatly with green ribbon. Catherine thanked the assistant and placed her items in the carrier bag she brought with her.

She made her way out of the delicatessen, but couldn't help but notice a young man, rather good looking, staring directly at her. This unnerved her slightly. He started to walk slowly towards her.

"Look, I'm sorry if I was staring at you just now, but you are Catherine Morgan, and I did see you at Braeside School earlier in the week?" the young man asked. "Yes that's right, and who might you be?" Catherine asked cautiously.

"Well, my name is Josh Fenton. I teach at Braeside school, have done for a while now. It's a tremendous and aspiring school, but I think we are in desperate need of an influx of new blood, new ideas and new energy. I do hope you were offered the position Catherine." She looked at the young man standing in front of her. He seemed on the face of it, rather presumptuous or was he genuinely interested in her joining Braeside School? Difficult to tell she thought to herself.

"Yes I've accepted the job. I start this coming Monday," Catherine replied.

"That's great, I'm so pleased," Josh said.

"Well, it's been nice meeting you Josh. Any tips or hints you could give the new girl?" "Not really, I think you'll fit in very well. The

Headmaster is a relatively newcomer himself. He's only been with the school for six months – making strides in the right direction though. 'Thorough and fair,' I would say."

"Well, I'll see you Monday, unless you would like to have a drink with me tonight at the Duke's Head in the Bay." Catherine was rather taken aback. She didn't know quite what to make of Josh. Hesitating, a little unsure of his slightly arrogant attitude, but thinking what harm can one drink do? She replied rather tentatively, "OK, what time?"

"Cool," Josh replied. I could meet you there or pick you up at about 8 pm?"

"No, please don't worry," Catherine replied. "I'll see you there at 8 pm tonight, at the Dukes Head."

"Look forward to it." That said she watched him disappear and walk slowly to his parked car.

Catherine stood outside the supermarket, in shock. What had just happened? What had she agreed to? Slightly puzzled, she made her way to the car, unloaded her shopping into the boot and set off for home, apprehensive, but a little excited at the same time. It had been a while since she had had a date. Her last relationship with Jeremy lasted two years, and had ended acrimoniously, so she hadn't wanted to put herself in that position again quite so soon.

***

Catherine pulled onto her drive and turned off the engine. She placed the handbrake securely on, sensing what was about to happen. There was no way of stopping it. She sat back in the car seat, prepared for the change that would gradually come over her and drifted away, somewhere else…

… She stood facing a large colonial-style residential house. The house had many shuttered windows, not unlike those seen in the most affluent of properties, scattered along the New England Coastline. All the windows overlooked the neatly kept and newly manicured lawns. It was a warm, still day, no breeze, not even the leaves on the trees surrounding the house had motion. There were a number of people milling about. A sign adorned the front of the house, but Catherine couldn't quite make out what was written on it. She walked slowly towards it, making her way along the cobbled path, getting closer and closer, trying hard to distinguish the writing on the sign. "I'm almost there," Catherine thought to herself...

Knock, knock!! Catherine was jerked back to reality. Focusing, she saw her next door neighbour standing by the car, knocking gently on the window. "Oh no, what a time for Mrs Busy Body to visit," Catherine thought to herself. She wound down the window. "Hello Catherine, I hope I didn't shock you? I have a letter for you. I had to sign for it, so I thought it may be of importance. What do you think it is? I hope you don't mind my bringing it over?" Catherine sighed in exasperation. "No, not at all Mrs Johnston, thank you," she replied. Mrs Johnston handed Catherine the letter, through the open window of the car.

Catherine sat motionless for a while. "What did I just see? Where was that place and how can I find out more about what I'm seeing but more to the point, why now and why me?" Catherine questioned.

Stepping inside the front door with her shopping, she placed the letter she had been given on the hall table, and decided to try and locate the school or university initially seen in one of her first visions. "This is never going to be an easy task," she thought to herself as she reached for her laptop that was resting on the sofa. She entered her password, typed in 'schools and universities with sports facilities and football grounds'. Catherine was almost sure the college or university was in the USA, so she researched USA. She was overwhelmed by the response from Google. "How am I going to locate this school or university out of the thousands it's showing me?" Having spent more than two hours perusing hundreds of sites, she decided to 'call it a day' until tomorrow, when she could dedicate more time and energy to the task.

Catherine closed her laptop and walked to the kitchen. Putting her shopping away, she sat down with a much needed cup of coffee and one of the iced cupcakes she had bought earlier at the local deli.

The time was now 5 pm. Making her way up the stairs and into the bedroom, she took her trainers and slightly faded black jogging bottoms out of the wardrobe. Quickly changing, she ran down the stairs and out of the front door, closing and locking it behind her. Remembering the letter on the table in the hall, she decided to open it later before meeting Josh at the Dukes Head. Catherine ran towards the sea at a fast pace along the promenade, and breathed in the sea air. It was bracing and invigorating as the wind caressed her face and blew through her long dark hair.

She hoped the run would clear her head sufficiently before meeting Josh later. Running at a slower pace now, she returned home, back through the narrow streets to her cottage. She opened the front door, and took the letter off the consul table. Fixating on the front of the envelope, Catherine looked at the redirection label, addressed to: Miss Catherine Morgan, Willow Cottage, Elm Lane, Port Isaac, but originally addressed to a Mr and Mrs M. Kruger – c/o Mr and Mrs G. Morgan, her parents address in Cambridgeshire. "That's odd. Who are Mr and Mrs Kruger?" Catherine spoke out loud.

Catherine pondered a while. She slowly opened the envelope. On reading the first paragraph, took a step backwards, holding onto the consul table for support, and continued to read the remainder of the letter, not believing what she saw...

Chapter 7
24 Years Earlier

The day of the enrolment for Yale University had finally arrived. Rachael and Susie shuffled their way slowly along the crowded corridor, full of would-be 'Yalies', waiting to get in line for registration. It took them a good thirty minutes to reach the front of the queue.

"Hi there, can I see your papers please?" asked the woman sitting behind the desk, as she slowly lowered her tortoise-shell spectacles. Rachael stepped forward and handed over her documents first. "Your identification documents also, please Rachael." The dark-haired middle-aged woman studied the papers for a couple of minutes before handing them back to Rachael. "They all seem to be in order. Thank you. And your documents please, young lady." Susie stepped forward and passed all her documents over waiting patiently as the administrator scrutinised her papers carefully for what seemed to Susie, a rather excessive time. "Well, yes, these are also OK," the woman replied. She collated the documents together and returned them back to Susie.

"For your future reference, my name is Jenny McGuire. I am the senior secretary here at Yale. You will both be in Davenport College. Each college is run by a Master and Dean – two professors, who live in the college itself.

"Within each college you will find a diverse tight-knit group that will make your academic experience unforgettable, as they have a good sense of community. In the basement of every college here at Yale you will find a cafe, yours is affectionately known as 'The Buttery'. It's a great place to break from studying and grab a snack.

Each college has its own student kitchen and library, and when you head downstairs in any of the twelve residential colleges, you will find an underground tunnel system connecting all the rooms."

"These are your keys. Do not lose them! There is a fine to pay if you do. So make sure you don't," Jenny McGuire confirmed strongly.

"Now if you follow the second year student with the blue badge she will take you to your dorm. It's room number 34B – first floor, where you can unpack and settle yourselves in. Here are several leaflets and maps that will help you find your way around the university and its facilities. They contain all the information you will need for this coming semester. If you have any further questions I will be here to help in any way I can. My office is at the front of the university, second on the left by the entrance. Good luck to you both and I hope you will be happy here at Yale."

Although Jenny McGuire came across as rather abrupt, Susie and Rachael thanked her politely and followed the student with the blue badge to Davenport College. The short walk brought them to the entrance of the college and they began to climb the steep flight of stairs which led to a long corridor with rooms on either side of the hallway. Following closely behind the young student they eventually reached room 34B. "Here we are, your dorm," the young lady confirmed. "If you need any further information please see Jenny McGuire. She will be able to help you." The Student left and disappeared quickly back down the corridor from the direction she came.

The dormitory was not overlarge, but adequate, painted pale lemon, with several interesting pictures that hung haphazardly on the far side of the room. The pictures and prints were mainly of the University in years gone by, but one print was of a large villa-style house. This picture stood out from the rest and was set aside from all the others. The Tuscany style villa had a creepy neglected old appearance, but would have been almost definitely magnificent in its day. There were two single beds in the dormitory, one small wardrobe and a wooden chest of drawers placed under the only window in the room. The curtains had a floral pattern and were tied back with corded tassels in bright red matching the small floral design of the fabric. The view from the window showed a large expanse of lawn in the centre of the college, surrounded by residential buildings all part of Davenport College, which made it feel safe and secluded.

"This is great, isn't it Rachael? Let's leave our suitcases and unpack later. We've plenty of time to explore, and find out where everything is, and in which buildings our lectures will be," Susie declared throwing herself on top of the nearest bed.

"Alright, come on then, but I don't want to be long, I want to get unpacked and organised," Rachael said placing her suitcase on the other bed. They locked the door to their room, being careful to hold onto the key, not wanting to feel the wrath of Jenny McGuire, and made their way back down the long corridor to the entrance of the college. "Shall we have a look around the grounds first and concentrate on finding all the buildings that belong to the university?" Susie asked. Where are those maps that Jenny McGuire gave to us Rachael?"

"Here Susie, you can navigate" Rachael decided and handed the maps to Susie, knowing full well map reading was not Susie best attribute. Rachael giggled out loud, and Susie acknowledged with a wry smile.

But they managed to locate most of the important buildings, and made their way back, down a leafy avenue to Davenport College. It was unusually quiet for the time of day, nobody about much bar a few cyclists on their way to the university. As they approached the end of the avenue, there, directly in front of them, on the corner of Hillhouse Avenue and Sachem Street, stood the Tuscan-style villa.

"Wow! This is quite something! Isn't that the old villa in the picture on the wall of our dormitory Rachael?" Susie exclaimed excitedly. "Why don't we go inside and look around?" she shouted as she ran across the road and up the steps to the front door. The door to the old villa was dark oak, impressive looking with a small leaded glass window in the centre, covered with a wrought iron casing. A highly polished brass plaque was prominently positioned on the wall near the door. It read: Horchow Hall.

The door was closed and a notice displayed which said: "Back in one hour."

"There doesn't seem to be anybody here, Rachael," Susie said disappointedly, peering intensely through one of the front windows. "We'd best come back tomorrow, eh?!"

Rachael glanced over at Susie. She was always amazed at her excitement, inquisitiveness and longing for adventure. "Sure, we'll come back when we have more time Susie," Rachael said as she pulled Susie out of the flowerbed under the front window.

Walking slowly back towards the College, they crossed the road, and looked back at the Tuscan-style villa. Why did the print of the villa have pride of place on the far wall of their dormitory, what was the history of the Villa, and what were its secrets, if any…?

Chapter 8
2010

It was 8.30 am. The sand was hot, even at that time of the morning, as Catherine stood at the water's edge. The warm sea lapped around her ankles like frothy soapy water, and the massive spans of ocean that extended out in front of her, was mesmerising.

She could feel her mobile phone vibrating in her jogging bottoms. "Hello, Catherine Morgan here."

"Good morning Catherine and how are you today?"

"Who is this?" Catherine enquired.

"My name is Joe. I'm calling from JDS, Wellington. It's regarding the PPI payment that is due to you."

"I don't have a PPI payment due to me, so please don't keep ringing me." Catherine replied defiantly.

"Yeah but, yeah but." Joe tried to continue the conversation as Catherine pressed firmly the red button on her I phone.

Catherine was kind and considerate but sometimes her temper and lack of patience got the better of her. A call that irritated her, selling something that she didn't want or a stranger calling her by her first name, was 'a red rag to a bull' as far as she was concerned. She felt a little guilty after ending the call, but nevertheless, it was done.

The early morning mist that clung to the roof tops of the small multicoloured cottages dotted along the coast had gradually disappeared. The tiny cottages looked as if they had been painted by an artist's brush, and Catherine had no idea why, but this always gave her a warm and secure feeling on her regular morning jog along the beach.

Arriving home she stumbled through the front door grabbing a small bottle of water off the consul table in the hall. Gulping it down as if her life depended on it, she made her way to the lounge and sat on her old comfy sofa. She began to read again the redirected letter she had received the previous day from the Swiss Bank.

"This can't be right!" she thought. "Someone has made a mistake. I'm not this Catherine Morgan? How can I be?" Again she read the penultimate part of the document out loud. "Your balance – with interest – over the last twenty-five years, held at this bank, now stands at $30,520,670! We have duly deducted all relevant taxes and would greatly appreciate your contacting us at your earliest convenience, as we note there has been little, if any, contact regarding this account, over the last twenty years. We therefore look forward to your urgent response to this matter. As the deposit is rather large, and the account has come to the end of its agreed term, we would like to discuss various investment options available to you. We look forward to your early reply… Yours sincerely…

She placed the letter back in its envelope, shook her head, not believing for one moment that the contents of the correspondence had anything remotely to do with her. "I'll ring Aunt Izabelle later. Perhaps she may know something, and she may be able to throw some light on the whereabouts of this Mr and Mrs Kruger?"

***

Michael Buble' was playing softly in the background. Catherine threw her sweaty jogging clothes into the dirty linen basket, and stepped into the steamy shower. The water was like a warm blanket engulfing her. She thought back to her date with Josh, and the unforgettable moment when he kissed her goodnight as he brought his mouth up to her lips and hovered there a while. The kiss was perfect and Josh was nice, but she had been there before. Could she take that leap of faith again, and would she like to chance another date with him? He had hinted that he would like to see her again, but there was always a 'but' when it came to her committing further. "Why can't I just say YES and take a chance?" Catherine spoke out loud.

"Mmmm!! Men are not my strong point. My relationships are like 'ships in the night', they pass by very quickly. What's wrong with me? I seem unable to sustain a relationship. Aunt Izzy always said I haven't met the right one yet. That always seemed a bit of a 'cop out' to me. I just want to meet someone I'm compatible with," Catherine declared, as she stepped out of the shower and wrapped a white fluffy bath sheet loosely around herself.

The all too familiar sensation started to well up inside of her. She started to wander outside of her normal realm...

Where am I? It's warm, balmy and feels like early evening. Catherine found herself outside a large villa-style building. Tall pillars each side of the front entrance led to several steps up to the large oak door. A light shone in one of the windows. Catherine felt the warmth of the late evening sunshine on her face. The villa was surrounded by overgrown plants and shrubbery, matured and parading around the many windows, not permitting the vast amount of light through that should be dedicated to each and every window of this magnificent house. It gave it a rather sinister and ghostly appearance...

Catherine moved closer along the stone jagged path, with its cracks only slightly visible as the 'world of weeds' pushed their way upwards towards the sky as if in defiance of gravity. This building was old, very old, and in desperate need of repair. "Where am I?" Catherine saw something ...

Then a phone ringing in the distance broke the silence! ... Catherine returned to reality and rushed to answer it.

"Miranda, it's you!!" Catherine replied.

"Are you ok Catherine? You sound strange," Miranda asked, sounding worried.

"No I'm a long way from OK! I've just had another vision and they seem to be getting more regular. I must see you. There's a lot going on right now, and I can't make sense of it." Catherine's voice wavered as she arranged to meet Miranda, at the coffee shop where they had met the previous week.

Drying herself, she dressed casually in a tracksuit, tied her wet hair back in a ponytail, grabbed her keys from the table in the hall, and left to meet Miranda.

***

Catherine pulled up outside the coffee shop in her Mini, locked the door and entered the café. Miranda hadn't arrived yet, so she ordered two cappuccinos and sat down at the table overlooking the harbour. Catherine didn't have long to wait. Miranda walked into the café with a worried look on her face as she approached the table where Catherine was seated. "Catherine what is going on?" Miranda asked. "You had better sit down, this may take a while," Catherine said as she showed Miranda the letter from the Swiss Bank.

"What's this? Are you this Catherine Morgan?" Miranda asked puzzled. "Have you got a rich relative somewhere?"

"Ha Ha, I wouldn't think so would you? It's either a bad joke or a complete mistake. I don't know what to make of it. I'm going to ring Aunt Izzy later, she may know something?"

"Are you still having those visions, or whatever they are?" Miranda enquired sympathetically.

"Yes, that's what's worrying me. They're getting more frequent and more detailed. I don't know what it is, I'm seeing. It's like I'm somebody else, if that makes sense. Like I am looking at somebody else's life, but through my eyes?"

"Have you seen anybody in these visions?" Miranda asked.

"Not really, but earlier when I stepped out of the shower, I had a vision. I saw a large villa-style building and seconds before you phoned, there was a shadow of a young woman, in the doorway of the house, standing staring at me..."

"Did you recognise her, Catherine?"

"I don't know, but she had long dark hair and what I could make out was that, she looked a lot like ME!"

The hairs stood up on the back of Miranda's neck.

"No!!! Where was this?" Miranda asked excitedly.

"I don't know, but I intend to find out," Catherine replied.

"How are you going to do that?" Miranda enquired.

"I did manage to identify the style of the building, a Tuscan villa, I think, very byzantine in its design; there can't be too many buildings of that type in the world – probably a few million!!"Catherine joked. They both laughed and thought of the task ahead as highly improbable. "If we can narrow it down slightly to an area, and a country of origin, then we have a better chance," Miranda stated.

Catherine thought back to the vision she had earlier. "I was standing on a pathway and the sun was warm on my face. It was early evening, I think. The shrubbery was somewhat tropical, so in all probability it was a warm and humid climate. I'm thinking it could well be somewhere in the USA or the Keys, or even the Caribbean."

They agreed to meet after work the next day, to start the search, and explore as many avenues as possible to find the Tuscan-style villa that had featured so prominently in Catherine's last vision.

***

Catherine returned quickly home from the café, entered through the front door, and placed her keys on the table and her bag on the small occasional chair. Although the hall of her cottage was not large, she had placed two beautiful framed prints of Kandinsky and Picasso on the far wall, which were a present from her parents, for her twenty-first birthday. These she would always treasure. They were one of the last things that her parents gave to her before their death.

Catherine walked to the kitchen and immediately dialled Aunt Izzy in the USA.

"Hallo Izzy, I'm sorry it's so late, I hope you weren't asleep."

"No dear, not just yet. Are you ok?"

"Well yes and no! I've received a letter from a Bank in Switzerland, the Credit Suisse Bank. It must be a mistake, but I thought I would run it past you, to be absolutely sure. It would be incredible if it was true, but of course, that's not possible."

Catherine read out loud the full transcript of the letter from the bank. "What do you make of it Izzy?" Aunt Isabelle stayed silent.

"Well! Do you know anything about it?" The silence lingered, but eventually gave way to Aunt Izzy's response.

"Yes dear, I do," Izzy replied.

Catherine was momentarily stunned.

"What do you know?" Catherine asked.

"The letter is authentic. The amount is probably correct after about twenty-five years of compound interest," Izzy replied knowing full well what Catherine's response would be.

"What!! Are you telling me I am this Catherine Morgan and I am about to inherit this $30,520,670? But why and who are Mr and Mrs Kruger?"

"Catherine, listen to me, listen very carefully. You must not tell a soul about this letter, not even Miranda. You may be in grave danger if you do. Do you understand Catherine?" Izzy strongly confirmed.

"No I don't. What do you mean by danger? You're scaring me. How can I be in danger, I'm a school teacher, living in Cornwall!"

"I knew this day would come eventually dear. But you can never be completely prepared for something like this. I will explain everything to you when I come over next week. I cannot talk on the phone, it may not be safe. You must keep this letter safe Catherine and I will see you next week dear."

"No wait Izzy, please tell me now."

"No, next week, all will become clear." Catherine promised Izzy not to speak of the letter to anyone, but she had already confided in Miranda. What harm could that do?

Aunt Izabelle replaced the receiver, and stood motionless in total numbness. She gazed out of her bedroom window at the full moon. It seemed to change the look of all in its path in an eerie and unpredictable manner as its light manifested a ghostly apparitional haze across the sea's surface and out and beyond... And so it begins...

Chapter 9
2010

The early morning journey to Braeside School for the start of Catherine's first day teaching was slow and thoughtful; she noticed little of her surroundings except the seagulls that flew low and hovered overhead. Their journey, unlike hers, was swift and decisive.

As she entered through the large wrought iron gates approaching the driveway to the school, her nerves began to get the better of her. She could feel her mobile phone vibrating in her jacket pocket, and pulled over to the side of the driveway to take the call.

"Hi Catherine, its Josh I just wanted to wish you good luck for today, and if you need any help, just give me a shout."

"Great, thanks Josh, that's kind of you, I'm certainly nervous, but I'm sure the children will make me feel welcome, and not give me too hard a time on my first day," Catherine replied. They both laughed at the very idea, and Josh said goodbye. Catherine's mind obligingly wandered back to that lingering kiss with Josh, which seemed a lifetime ago now as she drove up to the front of the school and into the car park. There on the wall in front of her was a small shiny brass plaque with her name delicately inscribed on it. Smiling to herself she drove straight into the space. The plaque was quite insignificant in the scale of things but it made Catherine feel quite important and she was eager now to meet the children in her class and to start her first day of teaching at Braeside School.

She entered the school through the main entrance and headed straight for the administrator's office. There were lots of children running about in the corridors considering the earliness of the day.

"Probably boarders on their way to breakfast," Catherine thought to herself, as she manoeuvred her way around the children and down the long corridor to the office. The Office door was closed. The sign on the door read: Mrs Palmer – School Administrator. Catherine knocked tentatively and entered without waiting for a reply.

A middle-aged woman with short dark hair was sitting behind a large oak desk. The desk was completely covered in papers and leaflets and you could hardly see the well-worn surface of the desk. She was on the phone, and involved in a heated conversation. Catherine noticed two slices of toast and marmalade that the administrator had tucked away, half eaten behind her computer, and a cup of steaming hot tea that was placed precariously close to the keyboard.

"Oh! Hallo dear, please take a seat and I'll be with you in one moment." The administrator continued her conversation. She didn't seem to be getting on top of the conversation and after several moments she slammed the phone down. Her face had turned a dark shade of red. She took a deep breath, a large gulp of tea, and tried to calm herself.

Catherine approached her desk. "Are you ok, you seem a bit upset? Can I help?" Catherine asked.

"No dear" I'm fine, really I am. It's always the same the first day back to school after the summer break. People let you down you see, and I have to try and pick up the pieces! I hope I didn't shock you," the administrator said, reaching for a tissue.

"No, I quite understand" Catherine replied, handing the box of tissues across the desk to her.

Mrs Palmer took the necessary documents from Catherine, and gave her everything that she needed for her first day of teaching.

Catherine already knew the curriculum. She had studied it intensely, hoping she'd left nothing to chance.

The first day went well. The children were a pleasure, not too disruptive, and Josh had been a great support during the day.

Catherine gathered up her belongings and took the coastal road home, which gave her time to think, not just about the day but about Josh and what that kiss meant, if anything. "Maybe it meant more to me than I imagined, or was I just fooling myself," she thought?

Sleep eluded Catherine best part of the night. Eventually she fell into a restless sleep. Her head sank into the pillow of goose feather and down which now felt hard and motionless.

She tossed and turned and wrestled continually until she drifted and drifted away... She found herself pushing open two heavy glass doors and walking into what looked to be a wine bar or club... A smoke filled room buzzing with the sound of jazz musicians; their instruments playing softly and melodically... "Hi Babe," said a young man who approached Catherine. He took her hand and pulled her to a small intimate table, lit by a single tea-light candle, which glowed through a small blue glass bowl, throwing a misty haze across its path. He kissed Catherine gently and passionately. Catherine could feel the heat of his kiss, lingering, warm and sincere with a passion she had never before felt. It took her breath away. "I can almost feel him. Who is this guy?" The waiter approached. "What would you like sir," he asked. "Two margaritas please, one with ice and one without," the young man replied.

A shadow of concern darkened Catherine's thoughts. How did this young guy know my favourite cocktail was a margarita? "That's too much of a coincidence," she thought. She looked around for anything familiar, anything at all that would help convince her she wasn't losing her mind!

Over in the far corner of the club the jazz band played. The saxophonist's fingers glided effortlessly across the instrument producing an almost magical sound. The pianist who accompanied him was note perfect. His fingers floated over the black and white keys, in a precise shadowing of the saxophone player.

"It is intoxicating here," Catherine thought, feeling, oddly enough, quite at home in the surroundings, protected by this strange young man. Have I been here before? The melody was familiar. Catherine tried hard to decipher the tune. She felt emotional, as the slow melodic rhythm began to overwhelm her. "I know this song – it's 'Stranger on the Shore,' Acker Bilk. Yes, that's it," she almost shouted out aloud in her sleep. "But that was way back in time, maybe the 1960s?" Catherine thought to herself.

"Could all this be relevant to me? Or am I seeing this through somebody else's eyes?" as things began appearing a little clearer to Catherine.

Hanging on the wall behind the jazz group was a display of large framed black and white photographs. They could well have been famous musicians who at some time in the past had visited the bar. On the adjoining wall was a huge blackboard. The white chalk drawings on the board of the jazz musicians playing in the club, were so lifelike, it was not hard to see why this artist was commissioned for his work.

"Hi Guys!!" Catherine turned to see a tall blond boy, about twenty years of age, who had approached their table. "Have you seen Susie? "I have something to tell her," he announced...

Catherine woke with a start. It was 6 am. Sweat ran freely down the front of her pyjamas, and the truth had evaded her once more. A single tear left her eye and trickled down her cheek as she sat in silence.

"Where 'on earth' was I? Who were those boys and who is Susie?"

Catherine realised it was now time to seek help.

She tried hard to recall the inscription on the heavy glass entrance doors to the club. She remembered pushing the doors open, and tried to think what it was that she saw inscribed on the doors. "I know there was writing on the doors and I'm sure the writing was in gold" ... "It was something to do with the colour blue," she recalled... "The Blue something ... The Blue Note Club" ... "Yes, that's it!! It was printed on the doors, in gold. I remember now – 'The Blue Note Club' (founded 1985)."

Catherine jumped out of bed, grabbed her lap top from the dressing table and typed in 'The Blue Note Club' and the year. "This can't be possible," Catherine murmured to herself, as more and more information began to unfold...

Chapter 10
24 Years Earlier

The weather outside was warm and sultry when Susie and Rachael arrived back at the dormitory, a little wiser and a little more aware of their surroundings.

The dormitory inside was hot and oppressive. The sunlight had entered through the window and had lingered long in the room. Rachael headed straight for the window. She opened it wide and felt the late morning air circulate around the dormitory.

They quickly unpacked their belongings as best they could in the limited storage space that was available to them. Unpacking done, they agreed to find the 'Buttery' and have a spot of lunch. The Buttery was advertised on one of the leaflets given to them by Jenny McGuire on arrival and was described as a 'rather good place to eat' and well worth a try. The dormitory door locked securely behind them, they head towards the Buttery.

In the crowded hallway, they noticed that most dormitories on both sides of the corridor were slowly being occupied. The air was alive with excitement. There were students rushing here and there in every direction in an effort to find their rooms.

Susie and Rachael walked to the far end of the corridor. Directly in front of them they could see a student struggling to hold onto the books and papers that were enveloped in her arms. They all inevitably fell to the ground hitting the floor, sending them sliding and scattering in all directions. She bent down hurriedly trying to retrieve them, as oncoming students attempted to avoid her and all the items splayed around. "Come on Susie, let's give her a hand," Rachael insisted, pulling Susie reluctantly over to help the girl gather her belongings together.

"Gosh. Thank you, I'm so clumsy you know. My name is Clara. I think that's why my friends call me 'Clumsy Clara'."

Rachael and Susie look at each other laughing at Clara's joke, before introducing themselves. Clara was a well-built girl, but not unattractive with long brown hair and stunning bright blue eyes which were by far her best feature. She had a jolly disposition and an easy laugh that was infectious.

The new craze that was sweeping the campus was her most treasured possession. It was a small tattoo of a butterfly on the inside of her ankle. You could tell she loved the butterfly tattoo and readily showed it to anyone willing to admire it. Clara thanked Rachael and Susie, and agreed to meet up with them later in the day.

The Buttery was relatively easy to find. The atmosphere inside the eatery was heavy with student chatter. An orderly queue began to form as the students bid to get closer to the food counter to place their orders for lunch. "Susie, you find us a table, if you can locate one. I'll line up and get us lunch. What do you want?" Rachael shouted.

"Perhaps a jacket potato with cheese and a coke," Susie shouted back as Rachael made her way over to the food counter to join the queue. "OK, I shouldn't be too long if the queue moves quickly," Rachael intimated to Susie.

In the meantime, Susie looked around the Buttery restaurant to find a free table. "Ah! There's one." She quickly made her way over to a free table in the corner and sat down, just in time before a group of boys attempted the same manoeuvre.

"Well done you," said the taller of the boys. "You got here a split-second before us, so I think that would call for me to introduce myself and my friends," he announced in a rather smooth way.

"My name is Todd and these two good looking dudes are my 'room mates', Danny and Brody." Susie looked up at Todd. "Gosh he's cute," she thought to herself. She was vaguely aware of her face flushing and hoped that Todd hadn't noticed.

"This is our first semester," Todd stated, "yours too?"

"Yes, ours too," Susie replied. "I'm here with my friend Rachael – she's over there – getting lunch, or trying to."

"Wow! Brave girl," Todd said. "You need armour plate to venture anywhere near that queue." Loud laughter resounded around the table. "Would you like to join us?" Susie asked. "I'm sure Rachael won't mind." They agreed and sat down at the table with Susie and waited for Rachael to return. Ten minutes later Rachael came back. Slightly seething, she steadily placed the tray down on the table, vowing never ever to return to the Buttery between the hours of 12 and 1 pm!

"Rachael, this is Todd, and his friends Danny and Brody," Susie announced. "Hi, I'm pleased to meet you all," Rachael replied. "Which college have you been allocated to?"

"We're all in Davenport," Danny spoke, looking admiringly across the table at Rachael.

"What a coincidence, so are we. It's possible then that we will see a lot more of each other?"

Rachael was not unaware of the admiring glance Danny had given her. There was little doubt in her mind that he was good looking, in a rugged sort of way, with his dark, almost black hair, and his brown eyes, great physique and an added bonus, he seemed like a nice guy! Rachael knew that Todd had the looks. But Todd knew it. Anyone could see that he was completely absorbed in his own importance. Rachael disliked Todd from the start.

The lunch remained untouched on the table. They chatted endlessly, getting to know one another better and made arrangements to meet up later that evening at the Gantry Wine Bar. The boys said goodbye and discussed amongst themselves on the way back to their dorm, the likelihood of any future relationships with Susie and Rachael.

With Todd and his friends gone, Rachael and Susie ate their cold lunch in peace. Susie hesitated and waited for the right moment before broaching the subject, but knowing full well what Rachael would say.

"Well what do you think of Todd, Rachael?" Susie asked, rather tentatively.

"Do you want me to be honest Susie?"

"Mmm! As a rule you generally are. So go for it!" Susie announced.

"Ok then. Todd is undoubtedly very good looking Susie, but he knows it. I think he's not to be trusted. He seems arrogant, conceited and full of his own importance. Be careful Susie, he could hurt you. Don't get involved with him. I'm advising you as your best friend. You did ask me, and I am telling you. Please listen to me Susie."

"OK, OK, Rachael, thanks I'll bear that in mind," Susie said. She knew full well that her attraction to 'bad boys' became almost a challenge for her, and inevitably she always ended up getting hurt. "When is Susie going to learn?" Rachael thought to herself. She just hoped that she wouldn't get involved with Todd.

Taking a slow walk back to their dormitory, they heard a muffled noise of what sounded like someone sobbing, very faintly, but in distress. They continued further down the corridor towards the sound of the crying. The door of the dormitory was slightly ajar. They knocked and entered gingerly. Clara was sitting on her bed, phone in hand, sobbing uncontrollably.

"Clara. What is it?" Rachael asked, putting her arm around her shoulder to comfort her.

"I've been dumped by my boyfriend, on the phone!" Clara confirmed, and continued sobbing inconsolably.

"Oh no, we're so sorry Clara," Rachael said. "How long had you been dating?"

"Not long really," Clara sobbed, "about a year. But I loved him and I thought he loved me."

They stayed with Clara trying their best to comfort her, and after a lot of persuasion she agreed to go with them that evening to the Gantry Wine Bar and meet the boys both girls had met earlier at the Buttery.

Back in their dormitory, Rachael telephoned her parents. Shortly after, Susie followed suit and both girls agreed to keep in touch and call again when they were able.

They sat on their beds, and looked across at each other. "Are you looking forward to seeing the boys tonight?" Susie asked.

"Yes, Danny seems nice," Rachael replied. "Are you?"

"Yes, can't wait," Susie said looking out of the window and hoping Rachael hadn't caught a glimpse of the excitement in her eyes, on seeing Todd again...

Chapter 11
24 Years Earlier

All three girls approach the Gantry Wine Bar. As they enter through the heavy glass swinging doors, the bar was buzzing and alive with the chatter of students and lecturers alike, and a variety of local residents, all enjoying the surroundings and singing along to the local jazz group playing an old Ella Fitzgerald number. The piano accompanying them was following the sound perfectly and was playing in unison, softly and melancholically in the background.

"This looks like the place to be seen in," says Susie. "Yes, it's certainly full of life," Rachael and Clara agree.

"There's Todd, Brody, and Danny over the other side of the bar," exclaimed Susie, and they made their way towards them. They noticed approaching from the opposite end of the bar, a small thin man, probably in his early thirties, and looking as if he could benefit from a good workout in the local gym.

"Hi, pal," exclaimed Todd. "Long time no see – How are you Vince? You're looking good."

"Yeah, I know, I've been working out!" and they both laughed at the thought! Vince placed his rather shabby small grey and black rucksack on the counter of the bar. He wore a grey t-shirt, (possibly white in a previous life) with a black and silver transfer of Led Zeppelin slashed across the front. His jeans were cut off and fashionably frayed. On his feet he had tatty old brown leather sandals, but his smile was warm and engaging, although his teeth were tombstone in appearance, yellow in colour and the odd black filling was obvious with his full extended smile. His eyes were covered by blue mirrored sunglasses and his head by a Boston Red Sox baseball cap that had seen better days.

The girls pushed their way through the crowds and eventually reached the boys, saying their hellos, they were greeted warmly. "Hi girls and who is this delectable creature? We haven't been officially introduced as yet" said Todd, who always took the lead in matters of the opposite sex.

"Hi Todd," replied Susie, "this is Clara a new found friend." Brody immediately introduced himself to Clara, and she too looked a little smitten with him. "Would you like a drink Clara?" Brody asked sheepishly. Not wasting a moment, he took Clara by the hand, and steered her towards the bar, ordering two glasses of white wine.

"This is good Susie isn't it? It will take her mind off her last relationship, which, by all accounts, seemed doomed from the start," Rachael stated. "Yes, your right, looking good with Brody, hope she takes it slowly!" Susie replied.

Can I introduce you girls to "Vince the Video Man?" Todd said. "Hi," the girls replied. "Hallo girls. Can I interest you in a video of your choice?" Vince enquired. "Or if you are a little more 'broad minded', an adult movie, I have many of them."

"Mmm" – thank you, but, no thank you," Rachael replied rather sharply, "not on this occasion." Rachael wondered what Todd was into. Susie had better be careful with him. She realised Todd was somewhat taken with Susie as she with him. I'd better keep a close watch on them, Rachael thought to herself.

"Hello Rachael, Danny said, "it's nice to see you again. How are you?" "I'm fine," Rachael replied. "Let's have a quiet drink over there," Danny asked, "on our own, and we can get to know each other a little better." They walk away, leaving Susie and Todd together for the first time, and Rachael looking back – worried.

"Alone at last Susie," replied Todd. "You are a spectacular vision you know." Todd definitely had a way with words, and Susie could feel her face glowing as she realised she was completely under his spell, and this could be dangerous.

"What would you like to drink Susie?" "Could I have a Pena Colada?" Susie replied. "You certainly can." Todd ordered one Pena Colada and a bourbon at the bar and led Susie over to a quiet corner of the wine bar. Sipping on their drinks, Todd sidled up to Susie. He took her face in his hands, bringing their mouths together, slowly, pressing his lips to hers, gently kissing her, familiarising himself, lowering his mouth to her neck, kissing, and biting, and gently finding her ear. Susie pulled him back to her mouth, returning his kiss with a long-awaited passion, and lingered there not wanting the connection to end.

"Susie you are fantastic! I want to see you again," Todd said. When Susie had regained her composure, and unsure of what she was really feeling, and whether this to be such a good idea, she replied with hesitation. "Yes I think I would like that Todd."

***

Several months pass. All three girls develop a good relationship with their partners, but none as strong as Susie.

For Susie at least, this had now gone beyond a casual relationship. She had fallen head over heels for Todd. Once again, she had not thought of the consequences,

He too, in his own way, was quite fond of Susie, but little did Susie know, he was a 'player of the highest degree', had a bad reputation and had no intention of committing to anyone, at this stage in his life.

Todd's father was high in office – a senator, and his mother a barrister; both had high hopes for him and his future – running for office – just like his father before him.

Rachael's worst fear was now becoming a reality...

Chapter 12
2010

Daniel Adams graduated university with honours. He had finally decided to forge a career in the highly lucrative investment banking industry, like his father before him.

It had not been easy for Daniel. He was not what you would call 'a natural' for the banking profession, unlike his father, who had accumulated a vast wealth, knowledge and infinite wisdom of all means and measures of mankind, how to handle difficult opponents, and desperate situations that arose during his long banking career.

Daniel persevered over the coming years, learning fast and making a name for himself in the banking community, to the envy of his many colleagues. He worked his way steadily up 'through the ranks', passing from one Trading Bank to another in a very short time, increasing his status as 'the new Trader' to be wary of in the square mile. Rising high in the ranks he gained a great accolade in the banking world.

Daniel Adams, now the youngest member of the Board of Directors at the Credit Suisse Bank in Manhattan, was well trusted, well acclaimed and greatly admired in the community.

Arriving at work – his usual time of 8.30 am; he passed through the revolving glass doors, as he had every morning for the past three years, with his Starbucks' latte in one hand and his old trusted brown briefcase his parents had given him all those years ago, in the other.

"Morning Johnson," Daniel called out to the concierge sitting behind his solid maple desk. The affluent reception area had an outrageously extravagant large display of brightly coloured fresh flowers adorning the counter area and almost obliterating Johnson. He replied; "morning Mr Adams; cold enough for you sir?"

There was a nip in the air that morning, unusual for the time of year, and premature for early October, but bright and exhilarating.

Daniel pressed number 26 on the brass panel in front of him. The view over Manhattan still excited him as the glass elevator accelerated and sped up the side of the building – the Head Offices of Credit Suisse Bank. It reached the 26th floor in little or no time at all. Daniel stepped out of the lift and headed towards his office.

He was, as every morning, bombarded with "Good Mornings" from each and every direction until he reached his office. On the office door the brass plaque read: 'Daniel Adams – CEO' – which always brought a lump to his throat, to think what he had achieved in such a short time, and the opportunities he was given early in his career. "Somebody must like me up there," he muttered under his breath.

Daniel pushed open the glass door to his suite of offices. His secretary, in the adjoining room, entered with the day's correspondence.

"Morning Mr Adams." How are you today?"

"Well, thank you Louise. And how is your little brother, is he out of jail yet?"

"Yes, eh… thank you for asking. The black sheep of the family you know," and they both laughed.

"Good, we can now get that interview arranged as soon as possible Louise."

"Thank you Mr Adams, thank you so much for this opportunity for Jacob, he won't let you down, I will make sure of that."

"I know he won't, he deserves a chance," Daniel replied.

Louise, Daniel's secretary, had had many jobs within the bank since leaving college. She had started her working career on the typing floor, document typing. 'Monotonous and soul destroying' were her words to describe her short stay there. She progressed through several other positions in the company until Daniel noticed her three years ago, working then for another colleague and had managed to persuade him, reluctantly, to pass her over to him to be his secretary on his appointment as CEO. She had worked for Daniel Adams ever since. They have a close working relationship.

Louise, a bright, accomplished and efficient girl, was small, about 5'3" tall, with a good figure, pleasant face and beautiful long blonde hair. Her little brother aged eighteen, was sent down for a twelve-month term, charged with shop lifting CDs and DVDs from a well-known chain store and selling them to his friends. He had quite a lucrative 'business'; that is until he was caught!

Daniel Adams had seen the potential in him. He was not a bad young man. He reminded him very much of himself at that age, just needing guidance in the right direction. Daniel decided to give him a chance for a better future, and arranged an interview for Jacob, downstairs in the back office, just as soon as he was released from jail.

Daniel pulled his black leather swivel chair over to his desk. The desk was large and impressive with a dark brown leather inlay, and solid brass handles to its many drawers. Two silver edged photo frames, stood next to each other on the left hand side of his desk. One photograph was of his family; mother, father and brother, and the other of a dark-haired girl in her late teens.

The office was large and spacious. The view from the floor to ceiling window achieved a vast vista over the total region of Manhattan – quite spectacular and breathtaking.

Apart from the large desk residing in the centre of the office, there was little else in the way of furniture, except a smaller mahogany side unit against the far wall, over which hung an extremely large painting. The painting, an original Kandinsky, "oversized and overpriced," was how Louise described the artist's picture, recalling the price Daniel had paid for it several years ago at auction.

Daniel started to peruse the opened mail on his desk. One letter in particular attracted his attention. He spent several minutes reading the document. The letter was from their Swiss branch. His thoughts lay on the surface of his mind, not penetrating, not allowing them to penetrate, but stirring dark and hidden memories, with just one name. 'Kruger.'

The contents of the correspondence to Daniel Adams were nonetheless intriguing... "The information given herein is with regard to a very large account in the name of Mr and Mrs Kruger – now deceased. The amount of $25,000,000 plus interest – totalling $30,520,670, is being held in trust for a beneficiary in the name of Catherine Morgan, dependant on her surviving her twenty-fifth birthday, and thereupon paid in full, on this said date." Daniel took out a pen from its container on the right-hand side of his desk, and twisted the pen between his fingers, nervously. He always found himself doing this when nerves got the better of him or thinking profoundly. It seemed to help.

Pressing the intercom to his secretary's office; Louise answered. "Yes sir?" "Louise, I want you to get hold of John Colbert at the FBI. His name is in your address book, and then put him straight through to me." "Very well sir." Daniel replaced the receiver and awaited the call.

Several minutes passed. The phone rang on Daniel's desk. He answered, "Daniel Adams." "Hello stranger," replied the caller, "It's John Colbert. How the devil are you?"

"Hi John," thanks for getting back to me so soon, I'm very well, and yourself?"

"A few aches and pains but nothing to worry about. What can I do for you?"

"Look I've had a letter from our Swiss Branch and it's rather baffling me somewhat. I would email it to you, but I'd rather not. I wanted to contact you first before any further correspondence changed hands. Do you understand?" Forcing a silent pause, Daniel continued. The caller now had his full attention. "The letter is regarding a couple called Kruger, and it's their deposit account at our Swiss Branch, of, wait for it, $30,520,670 that is slightly unexplainable, regarding its mystery recipient. Mr and Mrs Kruger are now deceased. This I know. The reason I know this John is because I knew them and their daughter, many years ago.

"What I would like you to do is find out more about the now beneficiary – namely a Catherine Morgan, who is apparently set to inherit the money, upon her twenty-fifth birthday, which I believe is imminent. The original recipients were her parents, Mr and Mrs Morgan, but according to this correspondence, they were killed in a road accident two or three years ago.

"I know this is not something you would take on lightly John, but I would deem it a great favour if you could look into this for me. It is somewhat personal, and I would be calling in the favour you owe me. Do you remember 'Melatone Electronics' two years ago, that little windfall you had...?"

"Yes, yes, ok, ok," John Colbert replied. "I will look into it, but please don't send me any electronic communications regarding this matter. It will be just between you and me, until you can work on your own with this one, ok?"

"Great! Thanks John." They conclude their conversation.

Several days pass. The phone rang on Daniels desk. "Mr Adams. It's John Colbert on the line for you." "Put him through Louise."

"Hi Daniel, I've found several pieces of information that I think might be of great interest to you..."

Chapter 13
2010

Catherine sat mesmerised in front of the screen of her Dell Laptop. It was showing her the 'Blue Note Jazz Club' in all its glory! The picture she saw was of the double glazed doors, with the 'Blue Note Club' sign handwritten on one side, just as she had remembered in her dream the night before. It stated that the club was just a 'short hop' from the many famous buildings, houses, and faculty departments, belonging to the Yale University and a popular venue for students and lecturers.

Scrolling down the page she came across a large number of photographs - many of the famous buildings previously mentioned. There were so many, too many to absorb, diverse in architecture and period, and others dating back hundreds of years but some more recent and modern in design.

Continuing her search, Catherine located an old building, so familiar in its structure, and yet unyielding in many ways, but it stirred past memories for Catherine, memories that were long forgotten. The house she had painted, as a child, all those years ago, was there staring her in the face! She sat back in disbelief.

***

The next working day came and went in a blur. Josh had phoned her mobile several times, but it remained unanswered. Catherine's mind was in complete turmoil, and she was beginning to feel unable to cope with day to day living. Oh no! Miranda's calling round after work! I'd forgotten all about that. Catherine jolted into action.

Sitting outside Catherine's house, Miranda sat and waited patiently in her small silver hatchback car for Catherine to return home from work.

Catherine was totally unaware of her haphazard driving along the narrow winding road, as she travelled much faster than the law allowed. It was a dull day. The rain poured down from the heavy dark cloud filled skies, randomly attacking the windscreen like a hail of bullets. Catherine finally arrived home. She drove into her driveway, and skidded to a sharp halt.

"I'm so sorry Miranda," she called out racing towards her as her feet met the many puddles on the surface of her driveway. "I completely forgot you were coming over today." "Don't worry; I knew you would be here eventually. I've known you long enough Catherine Morgan, and 'time keeping' was never one of your strong points." They laughed and made their way quickly, through the rain towards the front of the house. Catherine turned the brass key in the lock and walked in through the front door...

Both Catherine and Miranda stared straight ahead to the ensuing horror that awaited them. The chaos was unfolding in front of their eyes as they ventured further into the house. "What's happened Catherine? Did you not pay your cleaner last week? "Very funny Miranda," Catherine gasped, trying to hold back the tears. "No, it looks like I've been burgled."

They made their way to the kitchen, stepping over endless objects, cushions, magazines, and papers, all scattered around the floor. "We had better call the police Catherine," Miranda spoke out, looking around at the debris. "Has anything been taken? What were they looking for?"

Catherine had done exactly what Aunt Izzy had told her to do. She hid the letter, but not before acknowledging its contents to the bank in Switzerland.

"This must be something to do with the letter from the bank Miranda."

Catherine ran upstairs, narrowly missing the upturned chair on the landing. "Oh no, more mess," Catherine acknowledged. "This is going to take me forever to straighten," she thought to herself.

She headed straight for the bathroom. Just behind the white pedestal enamel sink, there was a loose tile near the base. Catherine had meant to fix it with grouting for some time, but never quite got around to doing it. She gently eased it out of its placing, and safe and secure, directly behind it, was the letter. Thank God for that!! It's still here. "This is what they were after. I know it! All they would need is personal details about me, possibly date of birth, mother's maiden name, passport number, all the usual details and in all probability, if they had this letter it wouldn't be too difficult to find. Almost everything they need to know about me is here! The rest would be relatively easy if you had the right contacts."

Catherine walked downstairs, letter in hand. "This is the letter I was telling you about last week Miranda."

Miranda took the document from Catherine. She saw the letter heading read: 'Credit Suisse Bank'. The bank was a well-known large bank. Its global head office was in London, but it had many European branches, and international offices scattered all over the world. Miranda knew this as she also had an account with this bank, opened for her by her parents many years ago.

"Catherine! Is this for real - $30,520,670?"

"Do you know, I really don't know," Catherine replied. "I'll know more when Aunt Izzy arrives here at the end of the week. She wouldn't tell me anything over the phone, she just warned me not to tell anyone and keep the letter safe."

"Goodness!! If this is correct, you are one rich bitch!"

"Don't be facetious Miranda," Catherine said, "I'm in a constant state of crisis right now, and I'm not sure who I can trust."

"Well you know you can trust me," Miranda replied.

"I know, you're a good friend to me," Catherine said. "You always have been." Giving each other a friendly hug, Catherine put the kettle on and wondered what to do next. There's no problem that a good cup of tea, or a glass of Sauvignon Blanc, can't solve! They laughed softly and tentatively.

After searching through all her belongings, strewn around the house, Catherine was fairly sure nothing was missing, as far as she was aware.

"If I report this to the police, there's no way we can mention this letter," Catherine divulged. "What do you think Miranda?"

"Yes you're right. That would really complicate things," Miranda agreed.

"But first I'm going to call Aunt Izzy in the States." Catherine picked up the phone and dialed Aunt Izzy's number. "Hello, who is this please," was the reply.

"Aunt Izzy, its Catherine."

"I've got a little problem," Catherine responded slowly. "Are you sitting down?"

"Yes dear, what is it?" Aunt Izzy sounded nervous and concerned.

"I've been burgled."

"What, when?!" Aunt Izzy replied.

"I've just got home from work. I walked through the front door, and found the house had been ransacked."

"Oh no dear Aunt Izzy replied. Have you called the police and more importantly, did you hide the letter? You're not hurt are you dear?"

"No, no I'm fine. I wanted to speak to you before calling the police, but I did hide the letter, just as you said, and it's safe. I think whoever did this may well have been after the letter and its contents."

"Yes you are right dear. Make sure you put it back in its hiding place, and then call the police. Is anything missing?" Aunt Izzy questioned.

"Not as far as I can tell," Catherine replied. "I'll check again before the police arrive. I'm really looking forward to seeing you at the weekend. I need to know everything Aunt Izzy, and I have so much to tell you."

"I'm looking forward to seeing you too Catherine and finally it's time that you knew the truth about your past. Goodbye dear. I'll ring you from the airport."

"Bye Aunt Izzy, see you at the weekend." Catherine replaced the receiver, and dialled 999. "I would like to report a burglary"...

Chapter 14
24 Years Earlier

Rachael stood in the early morning sunshine waiting patiently outside her parents' house for Danny to arrive. She didn't have to wait long. It was high summer and the semester had finally arrived, long awaited and long overdue. They had planned a day at the beach together, taking a slow drive along the coastal road – their destination – Long Beach – a popular resort with all generations.

Danny arrived uncharacteristically early at Rachael's house. He had decided to initiate an early start, to make the most of their day, as they achieve precious little time together as a rule, and he had something very important to say to Rachael, before the day was out, if he could find the courage and the right moment to do so. He pulled up outside.

Rachael's parents' house was a large new build, of brick and shiplap construction, a property that was pretty and appealing in design. There was an unusual weathervane that adorned the roof of the nearby separate garage block, that spun uninterrupted, creating a spectacular blur of colour as it rotated effortlessly in the morning breeze.

"Morning honey," Danny shouted from the car. "Hop in and we'll be on our way."

In the back of Danny's small green MG sports car was a large picnic basket, prepared by Danny's mother, and two large champagne flutes, for the Moët & Chandon champagne lying comfortably in its blue and red tartan picnic blanket. An icebox stood nearby. Inside were several bottles of white wine; Sauvignon Blanc and Pinot Grigio, keeping cool in their upright position, waiting to be consumed and enjoyed later in the day.

Rachael found it difficult to hide her excitement. She had developed a strong relationship with Danny over the last year at university. They both intended to keep it 'low key' because of the commitment they had made to their parents, and their hopes and inspirations of their future university degrees.

Rachael stepped into Danny's sports car and settled herself into the soft beige upholstered leather seat. Taking Danny's hand in hers, she moved slowly across and pressed her lips softly on his, for several moments longer than she anticipated. The feeling Danny never failed to give her was of warmth, security and an eerie calm that washed over her, with a strong notion of 'coming home' each and every time they kissed. He was her 'soul mate'; of this she had no doubt.

Danny's response was overwhelming and unexpected. Silence fell between them for a split-second. "I love you, baby," Danny whispered. "I can't hold back these feelings any longer. You don't know how you make me feel, sweetheart. I have never felt this way about anyone before." With that, Danny pulled Rachael close. She felt his strong arms wrapped around her, not allowing her freedom, kissing her passionately, and with longing.

Rachael responded with equal desire, separating only momentarily from Danny in an attempt to slow her breathing, replying; "I love you too Danny. I still remember the first time I saw you – I'm still sold."

"Stay with me tonight Rachael. We can make some excuse to our parents?"

"My parents would not understand Danny, and I expect neither would your parents," Rachael replied half-heartedly. "Let's make the most of the time we have together, enjoy today, and see what tomorrow holds." Reluctantly Danny agreed.

He turned the key in the car's ignition. It spurted and spluttered; finding its life, exciting him to think of the engine's power, vibrating and pulsating beneath his feet.

They made their way down the coastal road towards Long Beach. The day was sultry; a slight breeze danced around as it swirled their hair, gradually picking up speed, they enjoyed the warmth of the morning air curling around them.

They arrived at Long Beach by midday. The sun was now high in the sky, and was becoming hotter as the day unfolded. Rachael was glad she chose a sundress to wear, rather than her usual jeans and t-shirt, and glad also she remembered the sunscreen, as already the sun had turned her skin a pale shade of pink.

"Shall we park the car and walk along the beach before finding a quiet spot to have the picnic?" Danny asked. "Good idea, it's far too hot to sit on the beach just yet, and the walk will give us an appetite for the 'wonderful' picnic your mother has kindly made for us." They laughed in appreciation.

Danny drove along the sea front before stopping in front of a beach bar. As luck would have it, he managed to secure one of the remaining parking spaces available. So busy was the location, as cars came and went in search of somewhere, anywhere, to park their vehicle for the day.

Danny locked the car doors with his immobiliser, took Rachael's hand and they descended down the weathered cobbled steps to the beach below.

The Barracuda Beach Bar was heaving with young and old alike. Several steps led up to the wooden decking and veranda that surrounded the bar. There was an old multicoloured jukebox sitting at the far end of the decking. It produced a variety of sounds, old and new, from its vast library of vinyl. The jukebox was surrounded by wooden tables covered in neat pale blue linen tablecloths, ready for the lunchtime customers. The waiters and waitresses were identically dressed in black shirts and trousers with white braces, giving the desired minimal bistro effect.

An abundance of small neon lights, trailed neatly around the roof of the bar achieving a soft mystical mood and projecting its multicoloured lights down to the beach below, and the ocean beyond.

The jukebox randomly found a disc; an old Elvis ballad was selected. It reverberated smoothly through the air, easily and softly resting on the ear, as a number of couples sat down at the tables for the lunchtime menu.

Taking off their sandals, they walked slowly alongside the ocean, running in and out of the water's edge, laughing and playfully dismissing each thrust forward into the water, as they ambled further along the coast line.

Time passed quickly. It was now late afternoon; they returned slowly, strolling along the beach, engrossed in each other, as if not another soul existed, just the two of them, locked momentarily in time. Walking on, the sun behind them now as it gently caressed their backs with the late afternoon sunshine. They arrived back at the Barracuda Beach Bar, and made their way up the many cobbled steps to the car.

Picnic and wine cooler in hand, they walked around the small cove in the opposite direction from which they had come. Finding an ideal spot to set down, Rachael laid the tartan blanket down on the sand. The remainder of the day was now warm and balmy, as Danny rested the picnic and wine cooler down on the blanket.

The music from the beach bar drifted infinitely around the bay, still echoing its sound, now somewhat softer and less audible, but nonetheless pleasant in the early evening sunshine.

Danny took a champagne flute and passed it to Rachael. Taking the champagne out of the wine cooler, surrounded by melted bags of ice, he twisted and turned the wire connection holding the cork in place, and gently levered it off, giving way to the ever familiar resounding 'pop' and overflowing champagne, catching Rachael's glass, and eventually finding Danny's. "I want to make a toast to our happiness together. Your beauty and my good looks and personality, are the perfect combination!" They clinked glasses and opened the long-awaited picnic basket. Danny refilled Rachael's glass, and they both laughed at his humorous toast.

It was now late evening. The many day trippers had long gone, leaving the beach deserted. The jukebox could still be heard faintly playing for its evening diners. The tune was the sultry, melodious and moody sound of Barbara Lewis, 'Baby I'm Yours', from way back when. Rachael and Danny relaxed and laid back on the soft picnic blanket watching the array of stars multiplying before their eyes in the sky directly above them. The full moon could be seen intermittently in the night sky, camouflaged only by the few rogue clouds floating across its face.

Danny pulled Rachael closer. Looking into each other's eyes Daniel smoothed and pushed Rachael's hair slowly from her face, leaving just a single strand that strayed softly across her breasts. His hand moved gradually down, removing the strand of hair, and one strap from Rachael's dress. Then the other, pulling gently down revealing her breasts, soft and white, the warm breeze caressing them and her nipples, hard in anticipation and longing. Danny found her lips, kissed them relentlessly, but with reverence, arousal not denying either, as he lowered his mouth. He kissed her neck, biting and nipping. His hand found her breast, fondling and pressing, first one then the other, until his mouth reached its target.

Rachael pulled Danny's lips back to hers, and kissed him with such passion, not wanting to breathe. Danny eagerly stripped Rachael of her dress, and threw it on the blanket with his clothes, only panties remaining for Rachael, but she was unaware and not caring, as Danny's hand went lower, and lower, penetrating, and Rachael feeling his arousal next to her, as the love was made that they had both waited so long for.

Chapter 15
2010

Catherine Morgan passed quickly through the ever-busy revolving doors of the airport entrance, and headed straight for the coffee shop.

Her drive to the airport from Braeside School had been strenuous and tiring, leaving behind in its wake, a long and arduous day, as she tried to avoid the volume of Friday night traffic that accumulated as a result of workers taking to the roads early, in an attempt to extend their weekend break.

Ordering a skinny latte and a muffin, she walked over to the only empty table available by the window. It overlooked aircraft neatly parked in rows on the tarmac, awaiting instructions from the air traffic control, to take up their allocated departure slots. Catherine glanced over to the arrivals board. Her tired eyes scaled down the long list of arrivals and eventually found Aunt Izzy's flight. Confirming her worst nightmare as the rather shrill voice announced over the Tannoy system: Flight EM5241 from London Heathrow will be DELAYED – estimated time of arrival 20.10 hrs.

She used the long delay to her advantage, deciding on a sanguine approach and hoping the delay afforded her enough time for marking homework and catching up with correspondence that was long overdue for her attention.

Catherine watched the aircraft slowly taxiing to the main runway in readiness for take-off. Her shoulders relaxed and weariness left her as she sipped on her latte. She was mesmerised by the continual 'comings and goings' of the airlines, that were promptly serviced by a multitude of vehicles, in an attempt to get them off the ground, as soon as possible, to make a quick turnaround for the aviation companies concerned.

Her mind wandered and drifted... suddenly she found herself inside what appeared to be a large family house. She ascended the sweeping staircase to a pretty bedroom, a neatly made bed and a large number of soft toys sitting comfortably on a pile of pale pink pillows.

On this occasion she witnessed an emotionally charged conversation between two young women. One of the girls had long dark hair, was dressed in jeans and a t-shirt, and appeared to be comforting the second girl. She put her arm tenderly around her shoulder, as the second girl sobbed, inconsolably into her handkerchief. She was dressed casually in a light coloured track suit. Her long auburn hair was piled high above her head, giving way to the occasional strand that escaped and trailed down the side of her neck, framing her pretty, but tear-stained face.

The words resound in the room. I'm pregnant! Choking the words out as best she could, in great distress, she tried to gain solace from the dark-haired girl in the hope she could give her a positive solution to the dilemma she found herself in. "We must tell your parents straight away you know Susie..." Catherine focused back to the airport and to the sound of the Tannoy as it broadcast the imminent arrival of the delayed flight, EM5241 from London Heathrow.

Becoming all but accustomed to these random visions, Catherine was the more determined to get to the bottom of what she was being shown and why. "At last I have a name," Catherine thought to herself. "But who the hell is Susie?"

Catherine finished as best she could what work she had managed to 'wrap up', and made her way towards the arrival gate.

She had expected a wait of at least twenty minutes, when the luggage did eventually arrive, thundering up and onto the conveyer belt as passengers scrambled to reclaim their suitcases. Many began to make their way through the customs area, spilling out into the constant "hustle and bustle" of the arrival lounge.

Catherine didn't have to wait long for Aunt Izzy to appear, carrying several plastic 'duty free' carrier bags, and pulling along behind her a rather large brightly coloured suitcase. She was dressed in a long flowing floral dress, which can only be described as 'bohemian' in appearance. A 'throw back' probably to her wild days of the 60s, Catherine chuckled, and worn over the dress was a short beige linen jacket. On her feet, a pair of trainers!

There was no doubt that was Aunt Izzy. Catherine ran up to her, giving her a hug, and took her bags, relieving her of the weight she had had to endure for the greater part of the journey.

"Hi Aunt Izzy, it's so good to see you. Was it a good flight, apart from the delay?" Catherine asked. "Yes dear, very smooth, not too bumpy, and it's wonderful to see you too. I've waited so long for this time to come, and at last we can sit down together and discuss everything over a nice cup of tea."

***

Catherine turned the key in her front door, and put Aunt Izzy's heavy suitcase down in the hallway. She switched on the small silver lamp that sat on the hall table, which immediately gave life to the hallway, as it spread its light with a warm and welcoming glow.

"This is such a pretty cottage dear. I expect you are very happy here and settling into your new life in Cornwall as a teacher," Aunt Izzy enquired, slipping off her well-worn trainers, and placing them neatly at the front door.

"Yes Aunty I am, and I have lots of friends at the school, one in particular, Josh, whom I'm quite fond of. The headmaster has been very helpful too, but there is something I'm missing about him, which lies slightly uncomfortable with me; I can't quite put my finger on it though. Anyway, we can chat all day tomorrow and catch up, but now bed calls. I expect you are shattered eh?" Catherine asked.

Catherine showed Aunt Izzy to her room for her two-week stay. The room was cosy but not small, with two cottage-style windows affording a wonderful view over the bay and beyond. The windows were dressed with colourful poppy-patterned blinds, and the bed was positioned under one of the windows. There was a pretty china jug on the chest of drawers to the left of the bed, containing a mixture of country flowers. Their faint fragrance twisted smoothly and delicately through the air and around the room.

"The room is delightful Catherine," Aunt Izzy said. "I will sleep well tonight, thank you dear," and they said good night.

Catherine's sleep was fretful. Her day tiring, with tangled thoughts that spun in her head, as she tried to dismiss the black fear that was swamping her, of what tomorrow may bring. Eventually sleep found her and she awoke the next morning, to the sun streaming into her room, softly massaging her eyes as she gradually focused her vision and thoughts, to the realisation and importance of this day, the day she had waited so long for.

Tired but eager for the day, she made two cups of tea and took one cup to Aunt Izzy with her favourite digestive biscuit. Knocking gently on the door she entered but her aunt was already up and making the bed. "Ah! Thank you dear." They sat for a moment on the bed chatting together, before making their way downstairs to the kitchen.

It was a beautiful bright morning as Catherine prepared a light breakfast of croissants with freshly brewed coffee and orange juice.

Aunt Izzy disappeared upstairs and returned with a large manila folder. She also had, tucked under her arm, a large box, delicately patterned, and embellished with gold hinges and a gold padlock.

They cleared away the breakfast dishes and sat together at the kitchen table. "This is your past Catherine and your future." Aunt Izzy started slowly to reveal the contents of the box...

Chapter 16
2010

Daniel Adams swung his black leather chair over to the floor to ceiling window in his office. He sat motionless, soaking up the panoramic view of Manhattan stretched out in front of him. It never failed to brighten his day as he wondered at the picture postcard view in front of him, of the splendid early evening sunset.

He listened intently to the facts that John Colbert was relaying to him – "Also you remember Daniel, you mentioned that you knew Mr and Mrs Kruger, from your university days," John said. "I don't know how well you knew them, but it turns out they deposited a sum of $2,000,000 in an account in the Central Bank in the Cayman Islands on August 6th 1986." A marked silence fell before Colbert continued. "I've made extensive enquiries, trying not to raise suspicions within the Bureau, but it seems this sum of $2,000,000 was paid to the Krugers from an anonymous source, and its origin, as yet, I've not been able to locate. The majority of the money was then transferred, the very same day, to an account at the Credit Suisse Bank in Zurich where it has remained for the past twenty-three years, accruing interest at a set rate, now amounting to $30,520,670, give or take a few thousand dollars. I believe investments were made successfully over a period of time, to achieve this amount. But I don't know how.

"I'm still pushing the boundaries to find out who donated the $2,000,000 to the Krugers, and for what reason. I'm hitting a 'brick wall' every which way I turn. There is something not quite 'kosher' about this pal. Do you want me to keep digging or is it best left alone?" John Colbert enquired almost whispering. "You may be opening a 'can of worms' here Daniel."

"One other thing before I go Dan. Did you know that the Krugers were killed in a boating accident on their return from the Cayman Islands? Apparently the boat exploded, and the bodies were never found."

"No, I didn't know that," Daniel replied. "I knew they died in an accident whilst on holiday, but the information about how they died was never revealed.

"So do we know who was responsible for the cover up, and what about Catherine Morgan?" How does she fit into all of this?" Daniel asked. "I don't know yet," John replied, "but I've got a feeling I'm about to. Am I right Daniel?"

"Absolutely correct buddy," Daniel replied. "We'll have to get to the bottom of this. There is something perverse here, and why only now has this come to light? Somebody is hiding something. I want you to go deeper and find out what you can about Catherine Morgan. Somebody out there knows what happened to the Krugers, and I mean to find out what it was. I would deem it a great favour if you could pull out all your resources on this one John."

"What, another fucking favour," John replied? "You do realise if I get caught we'll both be in deep shit Daniel."

"Well let's make sure we don't get caught then, eh John? Really, I do appreciate your looking into this. I will owe you one, big time," Daniel confirmed.

Thoughts and forgotten memories from long ago surfaced momentarily, disrupting his long found peace as they continued to dance in his head. "Ok Danny, I'll be in touch soon." The line went silent. John Colbert replaced the receiver and sat back in his brown leather chair. He took a deep breath in, and exhaled out, opened the manila file kept under lock and key, well hidden in his desk drawer, and wondered what exactly he could be getting himself into. He read over and over again, "The bodies were never found." The words stuck like Velcro in his mind.

John Colbert had worked for the FBI for the past twelve years. He was greatly respected within the Bureau, as a well-known investigator of some note. His office was small and somewhat shabby in comparison to Daniel Adams' luxury office, but adequate for his needs. His desk was made from oak veneer with a steel casing, with just one wooden photo frame pushed to the corner of the desk, which sat precariously on its well-worn surface. The photo was of his wife and child, a reminder of his past life before his acrimonious divorce five years earlier. The Bureaux had a lot to answer for. The remaining surface of his desk was totally covered with papers, documents, scraps of paper and whatever else John was working on at the time. His computer was all but hidden under the mound of files now piled up in his in tray, awaiting his urgent attention, but not finding it.

Focused, he forged forward, as he always did, and started with the Krugers and their life before the accident, their family and their home. It was no accident, of this he was sure. What happened on that day over twenty-three years ago?

John Colbert's cell rang somewhere on his desk. He scrambled across his desk and retrieved it from under a pile of papers, and answered. "Hi this is Colbert, what have you got for me...?"

The sun had now disappeared behind one of the many skyscrapers on the Manhattan horizon. It left behind a pink and orange halo, which gave rise to the onset of what could be a beautiful tomorrow.

Daniel sat for a moment, drawn into the view in front of him as his mind drifted back to his university days and the happy, carefree times he enjoyed with his university friends. What Daniel had lost to youth had he gained in sharp intelligence? He knew something would transpire from this forthcoming information, but what, he had no idea.

"I'm off now, Louise said. Is there anything you would like me to do before I go, Mr Adams?"

"No. No thank you Louise," Daniel replied. "Have a nice evening. See you in the morning."

Daniel Adams took a brand new white shirt, still in its cellophane, from the second drawer down in his office desk. He had left himself just 30 minutes to get to the Chase Manhattan Hotel for his 8 pm business dinner with the new CEO of the Staten Island branch. He had timed it to perfection, as he left his office, and jumped into the waiting cab. Daniel arrived outside the Chase Manhattan Hotel at 7.50 pm.

***

Daniel had never married. He was forty-one years of age on his last birthday, had had a string of girlfriends and several long-standing relationships, but nothing had come of them. His career was now his life.

His home was a penthouse on the outskirts of Manhattan, in a newly built apartment block. It stretched entirely across the fifth floor, and boasted its own rooftop garden with a mini plunge pool. Daniel stayed there during the week. Just a 'stone's throw' from his office, it afforded convenience for both entertaining clients, and travel to and from the bank. Prestigious and expensive was his description of the apartment, but it was not entirely to his liking or true to his character.

He also owned a further property in New England, lakeside, not over large, but beautifully designed, with a colonial appearance, original design, and was painted a pretty pale green colour. That is where you will find Daniel Adams most weekends, pottering in his garden, or sailing on the lake with his Sun Seeker yacht, aptly named, after the one and only girl he had truly loved and lost many years previous. He would give up everything for just one more day with her.

***

Daniel arrived at the bank early the next morning. He entered his office, his usual latte in one hand and briefcase in the other and sat at his desk, computer on ready for the day ahead.

It was 7.30 in the morning. Daniel's cell phone buzzed, denying him any chance of peace and quiet, "morning chum. John here." In a low voice John continued. "Sorry it's early but I thought you would want to hear what I've uncovered straight away. My source told me that the boating accident was no accident, of that he was pretty sure. You were right, there was a massive cover up, from high into the echelons of power, by all accounts, but just how high, we've yet to uncover."

"There is something else Daniel, which could be very significant. Someone else was on board the boat that day – twenty-four years ago. It was a baby...

Chapter 17
24 Years Earlier

Susie arrived fashionably late, unusual for her. She'd arranged to meet Todd at the old Tuscan villa on the corner of Hillhouse Avenue and Sacham Street at 8 pm. The time was now 8.15 pm. As she turned the corner, he was already there standing, waiting on the steps. He'd worn a white cotton shirt and blue jeans, showing off his amazing physique as he cupped his hands and lit a cigarette that showed the tip glowing red in the early evening light.

"Hi, baby" Todd said. "Wow you look great." He staggered momentarily as he took Susie by the hand and led her up the stone steps and into the villa. He'd had several beers and a couple of bourbons in the Blue Note Club with Danny and Brody before meeting Susie. He was slightly inebriated. The door to the old villa was locked when Todd arrived moments earlier; hurriedly he scouted around the rear of the house and found an unlocked ground floor window. Climbing through the window he made his way along the corridor to the heavy oak front door and unlocked it from the inside.

"Todd, are you OK?" Susie asked, genuinely concerned. She had never seen him wavering and swaying in this uncharacteristic way before. "Yep, I feel great. Come on let's explore this old villa a little. They say it's haunted you know," teasing Susie. "Stop it Todd, you're scaring me," Susie shouted, moving slowly backwards to the old oak front door. The dark shadows that Susie had sensed earlier seem to have escaped their hiding place and followed her in her retreat. "We shouldn't be in here at all Todd," Susie exclaimed. "We'll get into trouble if someone catches us." "Come on, don't be such a 'wus,' Susie, let's look upstairs," Todd motioned. He pulled Susie gently up the heavily carved wooden staircase and onto the first floor landing.

The villa would have normally been in complete darkness at this hour of the night. The full moon was now pushing its beam of light steadily through each window, giving the unusual appearance of daylight arriving early, covering each room with an eerie blanket of light. Susie reluctantly followed Todd from one door to another, until they reached a room at the far end of the corridor.

Todd beckoned Susie inside. The room was surprisingly small with unvarnished wooden floor boards that creaked under foot. There was a large circular faded Indian fringed rug covering the centre of the room, and opposite the door, a window overlooked the garden to the rear of the villa. A large double bed was against the far wall, partnered by one single side cabinet, and a small chest of drawers. A single floral upholstered chair sat comfortably under the window, and was complemented by identically patterned curtains hanging in the circular bay window. It was a pleasant room, if somewhat basic.

Todd pushed Susie further into the room. The moon's gaze entered the windows, bringing with it, formidable shadows. Todd pulled Susie down onto the bed. "No Todd, not here," Susie cried. "It's not right. Please Todd, NO." Todd took little notice, as his mouth pressed down on her lips, hard and fast. He tore at her top and ripped away her bra, quickly and sharply, leaving her partially naked, finding her breasts, he squeezed and bit until Susie cried out in pain; "please no Todd," but Todd was too strong. His hand travelled lower. He reached into her panties, ripping them away, pushing her legs apart, his erection now powerful, without a second thought or hesitation, he entered Susie. He was completely overcome with lust and desire thrusting relentlessly, he reached his moment.

Susie lay on the bed, for several moments, motionless, unable to speak, sobbing endlessly. It seemed so disingenuous; she had waited a long time for Todd to make love to her, and now all she wanted to do was get away from him.

"Come on Susie, you know you wanted it," Todd retorted. He pulled on his jeans and buttoned his shirt. "But I thought you loved me. I thought it would be different to this, and I thought you would be different to this," Susie sobbed.

"You knew it was never going to be long term between us Susie. It's been fun while it lasted," Todd stated coldly. "I think a lot of you, but I've got my career to consider, and my future."

"What about me Todd, don't I have a future as well as a career to look forward to?"

"You'll find someone and eventually settle down and have kids," replied Todd, uncaring and devoid of any sympathy for Susie.

Susie dressed as best she could. She stood and walked towards the door, sobbing. She turned to face Todd calmly saying: "I hate you Todd, you haven't heard the last of this, you bastard." She ran out of the room, down the stairs, tears streaming down her face, and into the cool night air.

***

The next morning arrived soon enough. Susie disappeared into the bathroom, bruises showing clearly now on her arms and legs, and however hard she tried, she couldn't hide them.

Rachael woke sleepily. "You're up early Susie, it's not like you. Couldn't you sleep?" "Ah, no, I thought I would make an early start, I've got so much reading to catch up on before the end of the semester," Susie replied, wrapping her dressing gown around her tightly hoping Rachael wouldn't notice any of the bruises.

Rachael stepped out of bed, stretched, and made her way over to the kettle resting on the side by the sink. "Do you want a cup of tea Susie?" she asked. Not waiting for an answer, she placed a tea bag in each of their mugs, and poured the boiling water in. She handed Susie a cup, with added milk and sugar. Rachael's eyes widened. "Susie, what are those marks on your arm?" Susie quickly tried to cover them. Rachael took hold of Susie's arm and pushed her sleeve up. "What happened to you? How did you get these bruises?" Susie slumped on the bed, too exhausted to lie, and too upset to render an alibi for her behaviour the previous night.

The tears slowly escaped her reddened eyes. They trickled down the side of her face and onto her clasped hands, resting on her knees that were tightly pulled up to her chin. "He raped me last night Rachael," Susie gasped. "I couldn't move; he was too strong for me. I think he'd been drinking. It was frightening Rachael, I'm so upset." Sobbing now, Susie hoped Rachael would have an answer to the horrific situation she found herself in, to make it right, but there was no answer. "It was partly my fault. We shouldn't have been in the old villa. I didn't want to go in. He pulled me up the stairs, as I tried to stop him, but he wouldn't listen. We shouldn't have been in there. I can't report it, God knows I want to, but if I do, we will be asked to leave the university, and I won't let that happen, what would my parents say?"

Rachael sat and listened to Susie, without interrupting. "You should report this Susie, why should Todd get away with it? But if you do, you're probably right, they may ask you to leave. I think we should go and pay Todd a visit, and see what he has to say, don't you?"

8 Weeks later

Rachael sat in the dorm, talking to Clara, planning a birthday surprise for Susie for the following week. It was Susie's nineteenth birthday, and they had lots of arrangements to make, not least the surprise striptease which Susie would hate, but would endure for the sake of her friends.

Susie walked unexpectedly into the Dorm. She was supposed to visit her parents, and not return until the following day.

"You're back early Susie? What's wrong honey, are you ok?" Rachael asked. She could see that Susie was upset. Susie broke down in tears. "I'm pregnant Rachael." Silence was the only sound in the room. Clara looked at Rachael in disbelief, and moved across the room to sit with Susie. "I don't know what to do," sobbing as Rachael comforted her, putting her arm lightly around her shoulder and trying to find out who the father was, but of course knowing, for sure, it could only be one person. "Have you told your parents yet Susie?" Rachael asked. "No. They will be devastated," Susie replied.

As a Catholic, it left Rachael in no doubt that Susie would not want to terminate the pregnancy. Susie sat staring out in front of her. "He is such a bastard. Firstly he raped me, and now he wants nothing to do with me or the baby. What am I going to do Rachael?"

"Firstly we need to pay Todd another visit. This time he cannot deny it, and you will need help from him, and then decide what you are going to do, regarding this pregnancy. You have got to tell your parents Susie. I know it won't be easy, but it has to be done, and the sooner the better for all concerned..."

Chapter 18
2010

Great Aunt Izabelle began to reveal slowly, the truth that had eluded Catherine all her life, and finally the facts began to emerge about her birth parents and their life before Cambridge.

"You were born Catherine Kruger, in Canada, on June 24th 1985 to the daughter of my dear friend Janet Kruger, Aunt Izzy began. Mike and Janet Kruger were our very good friends and neighbours. They had three children, two girls and one boy. All their children were academic, highly intelligent and each received a scholarship to the 'University of their Choice.' The youngest of their children was a girl. Her name was Susie."

Catherine sat for a moment, unaware of her surroundings, insentient and frozen into silence. "This really can't be true, can it? Did you say Susie, Aunt Izzy?"

"Yes, her name was Susie dear," she replied.

"But Susie is the girl in my most recent dream. It's the only name I have to go on so far," exclaimed Catherine. Izzy faltered, hesitated, and considered her words carefully before continuing.

"Catherine, I believe you have a strange and unexpected gift, which is only now beginning to manifest itself. Your mother also had this gift. The visions or dreams that you are experiencing are no accident of fete. You are seeing someone else's life, or moments in time of that other life, and your life now, is somehow connected to their life then."

"There is something that happened long ago in the past, a mystery, that needs to be uncovered and these dreams you are experiencing now, in the present, are for a reason that I think will enable you to seek out the truth."

Aunt Izzy continued. "Both Susie and her close friend entered Yale University on a scholarship, and were so happy to be entering the same university together. Janet and Mike Kruger's wealth was not as great as that of her friend's parents and they sometimes found it difficult to make ends meet, having three children at university at the same time was a great hardship and sacrifice for them. This was significant and will become more apparent as time goes on."

"They settled quickly into university life, and made many friends. There was Carla, whom I remember well. She was a delightful girl, friendly and funny, and always willing to help. Then there were the three boys, Todd, who paired up with Susie, Brody with Carla, and Danny with Susie's friend. Her name was Rachael. They all got on famously well together until that fearful day..."

The ringing of the telephone shattered any illusion of time. Catherine quickly left the kitchen and walked down the hall to answer the phone. Any distraction now would render her further away from gaining the truth of her past, and all that it held for her. Reluctantly she answered the phone and discovered that Braeside School wanted her to take a class for two hours, due to Mrs Sugden being rushed to hospital with an unexpected appendicitis. The school had tried all avenues open to them, to secure another teacher before approaching her as a last resort, as they were aware she had a guest staying with her, but they had no option but to make the call.

Catherine walked back to the kitchen. "Aunt Izzy, I have to go to work for a couple of hours to take a class. A teacher has been taken ill and they have nobody else to cover today. I shouldn't be too long. Will you be alright on your own for a while?" Catherine asked.

"Yes dear, of course. We can carry on where we left off when you get home."

"OK. If you are sure you don't mind, I'll see you in a few hours." Catherine kissed her aunt, grabbed her handbag, keys, glasses and jacket and headed for the front door.

As Catherine closed the front door behind her, an uneasy feeling crept over her. Nothing she could put her finger on directly, but nonetheless, unnerving.

A wide blue cloudless sky loomed up in front of her as Catherine drove through the winding country lanes. A never-ending abundance of wild flowers showing her flashes of colour, passed by her car window and after ten minutes she finally arrived at the entrance to Braeside School.

She saw Josh standing on the steps to the front door of the school, waiting for her. Catherine made her way towards him and up the short flight of steps. He extended a hand to her and pulled her towards him, pressing firmly against her body, and kissed her softly, but passionately. "Gosh I've missed you Catherine. Glad you could make it sweetheart. Do you fancy a drink tonight at the Horse and Dragon?" Josh asked. Catherine looked into Josh's eyes. A warm sensation greeted her. She knew she could fall for him quite easily. "I would love to Josh, but my aunt is over from the States, and she's only just arrived, another time soon, eh?" Catherine replied.

Catherine made her way to the Headmasters office as instructed. The door was slightly ajar as she approached the room. She could hear a muffled conversation between Martin Castona and Miss Galloway, nothing that she could decipher; the conversation slightly heated, but not hostile. Catherine knocked softly before entering.

Both the Headmaster and Miss Galloway appeared a little apprehensive, as Catherine entered the room. "Please sit down Miss Morgan. We have something very important to tell you, before you start your class. Be prepared; it may shock you..."

***

91

Chapter 19
24 Years Earlier

It was now early January and a slight chill hung in the air, but a bright and crisp day was forecast. The winter sun greeted the snow, transforming it into a white blanket of shimmering crystals, camouflaging the fields and meadows as the scene swiftly passed by the window of the car. Susie drove slowly home from university, preparing herself for the task ahead.

She pulled onto the driveway of her parents' home. The house was a moderate four-bedroom property, homely and well maintained. It had a red slate roof, and the wood that adorned the outside of the house was painted a pale blue, giving it a pleasant nautical appeal.

Stepping up to the front porch, Susie turned her key in the lock of the front door, and stepped inside. "Is anybody home?" she called out, not really expecting a reply, as both her parents were usually at work at this time of the day, but she was happy in the knowledge that there would not be too much of a wait before her mother returned.

Susie sat down on the well-worn brown leather sofa and glanced around the sitting room. The red patterned rug under her feet was now showing signs of wear and the furniture looked old and tired, but the photo frames of her family, scattered endlessly around the room, brought warm and comforting memories, making Susie feel safe and cosseted, as she closed her eyes and drifted into a fretful sleep.

"Susie, wake up honey." Her mother gently tapped her. "We weren't expecting you home until next week, but I'm so pleased to see you. I'll make us a cup of tea and I have some of your favourite homemade scones." Susie couldn't get over the way her mother still fussed over her as if she was still a child, but on this occasion she really didn't mind.

Susie woke slowly, stretching her arms as she tried to relax her shoulders in readiness for what she was about to divulge to her mother. Nervous, and her palms sweating, Susie slid back on the sofa, having no idea how her mother would react to the news. She was now three months pregnant, hardly noticeable at all and all trace of morning sickness had disappeared several weeks earlier, for which she was grateful. Butterflies fluttered in her stomach as she followed her mother into the kitchen. Her tea and scone were there on the pine table as promised and Susie sat down. "Mum I have something to tell you. Please sit down; I think you might need to."

Janet Kruger carried her cup of tea to the kitchen table. With trepidation, she pulled a chair away from the table and sat down waiting for Susie to tell her the news that every mother dreaded.

"There is no other way of saying this. Mum, I'm pregnant! I am so sorry." Susie's mother sat stunned into disbelief at the news she had just been given. Lost for words, all she could say was, "Are you sure Susie. Could you just be a little late?"

"What, three months late mum?" Susie choked. "I don't think so," she said, holding back the tears. "I'm pretty sure, having done two pregnancy tests. The father is Todd, but I expect you know that. He wants nothing more to do with me or the baby. I didn't know what to do. I've been so worried about telling you and dad, and so upset." Janet Kruger walked around the table and put her arm around Susie, pulling her close. "Don't cry Susie, I'll tell dad when he gets home, we can work it out and decide what is the best way forward with this. He will be upset Susie, I know he will, but it's nothing we can't handle together as a family."

Susie wiped away her tears and continued to tell her mother exactly what happened on that fearful day in September, and why they couldn't inform the university for fear of being asked to leave.

Janet Kruger was very disappointed in Susie the way things had turned out. They both had great hopes for Susie's future as she was so bright, academic and sterling in her ambition to succeed in whichever career she chose, but there would be no doubt that they would stand by her whatever happened.

"The first thing we are going to do is write to Mr and Mrs Clayton, Susie's mother confirmed, giving them the facts and ask for a meeting to sort out what the next step should be, and the financial help that you will need when the baby is born." Mrs Kruger had no intention of letting Susie have an abortion; they were devout Catholics; this was not an option for them. Susie had already realised this would be her fate, and that her parents would not entertain a termination, so she had resigned herself to having the baby, keeping it, or giving it up for adoption, at a later date. The adoption idea Susie had not thought through.

***

It had taken all of Janet Kruger's strength to stop Mike Kruger from going to the Clayton residence the following day and thrashing Todd to an inch of his life. The moment passed as Janet managed to convince Mike to calm down, and that no good would come of a physical confrontation at this point. Mike sat down in his favourite armchair, lit a cigarette, and drew deep and long, as he tried to make some sort of sense of the situation. He knew, as did Janet, that Todd probably had no intention of standing by Susie, if the ruthless reputation of the family was anything to go by. They were known, of course, for their accumulated wealth, and hostile action towards anyone or anything that stood in their way. Susie had been warned many times, by both her parents and Rachael, but stubborn as she was, love was blind, and Susie didn't want to know what would be in store for her in the future.

It was now Saturday morning. Susie was fast asleep upstairs and Janet and Mike were still in conflict over the previous day's news. "We must send this letter straight away Mike and hope for an answer from the Claytons pretty soon," Janet said. "This can't be left any longer, or we will have to contact the authorities, and register a complaint of rape against Todd."

"Let me see the letter you have written before you post it Janet," Mike said. "We have to be very careful as I bet the Claytons have contacts in high places and connections to unscrupulous persons, of which are probably on their payroll." Mike studied the contents of the letter and agreed it was straight to the point and would not be construed as offensive in any way. Mike admitted to himself, that

John Clayton, being a senator and his wife a barrister they would not want any untimely publicity at this point. John Clayton was currently running for office, and any past history that may 'come to light,' would not be advisable, or any problem which could affect the future prospects of their son Todd, they would not tolerate. Mike reluctantly agreed, as what else could they do to help Susie and the baby? He did not want to 'overstep the mark', or put his family in any danger. He finished his mug of black coffee and breakfast pancakes, and made his way out of the front door and into his black Chevrolet. Driving to work he had an uneasy feeling that this could turn out badly for them, if they weren't very careful.

Susie slept well that night, the best for many weeks, knowing she had at last told her parents the news she had been hiding for so long, and felt a great weight lifted from her shoulders. Pulling on her white towelling dressing gown and pink fluffy slippers, she made her way downstairs.

Yours sincerely

Janet Kruger

"Morning mum," Susie yawned. "Tell me, how was it with dad?"

"Just as I had expected dear," replied her mother. "I think he wanted to kill Todd, he was so angry. He's gone off to work now to calm down. We'll discuss it later this afternoon when he gets home."

This worried Susie a little; she knew what a temper her father had, and she didn't want him visiting the Claytons and making a scene, if there was any other way this could be resolved.

"I have written to Mr and Mrs Clayton, Susie," her mother said. "There is a copy over there, by the toaster, read it through and tell me what you think before I post it."

Susie picked up the neatly typed letter on home headed paper and started to read its contents:

Dear Mr and Mrs Clayton,

I am writing this letter to inform you of the unfortunate position my daughter is now in. I do not know if you are aware of what happened in September and whether or not your son informed you of which I very much doubt, but my daughter Susie was raped by your son Todd, against her will and is now pregnant.

Our whole family are very shocked and upset by what has happened, and do not wish to cause any more anguish to Susie than is necessary.

There is no question of a termination, as our religion is Catholic, and this is not an option for us. So we have decided that nearer the date of birth, Susie will visit her aunt in Canada, have the baby there and return home, when we shall then decide upon what course to take regarding the baby's future welfare.

In your social standing we understand you will not want any adverse publicity and therefore ask you to think very carefully what help you would avail to us, and a monetary contribution for Susie and the baby's future care. This would be long term for the period up to and including university fees. Therefore if you agree on one final payment, this should be substantial.

I look forward to your reply as soon as possible.

Yours sincerely Janet Kruger

"Wow mum. That is some letter. Do you think they will go for it?" Susie said with relief. "They will have to help us, or take the consequences, Janet replied, sealing the envelope securely, and placing a stamp in the right hand corner. "I'm off to the post box now Susie. There are some pancakes and coffee on for breakfast, help yourself, I won't be long darling."

Susie read the letter once more. A niggling thought entered her mind. "This could get complicated. I do hope mum and dad are doing the right thing and so do I…"

Chapter 20
2010

Catherine returned home from Braeside School. She had been asked by the Headmaster, to cover for Miss Sugden, who had been rushed to hospital with an unexpected appendicitis. She hadn't remembered driving best part of the way home, as her mind was somewhere else, and no other thoughts had priority at that time.

The information that both Miss Galloway and Martin Castona had confided to her was so unexpected and unbelievable; the fact that she was sworn to secrecy didn't help, as she wasn't able to divulge any part of it to her aunt. This would prove particularly difficult as Aunt Izzy was just starting to make known to her, her life before Cambridge, and how she was adopted, and more importantly, why.

"You weren't too long dear," said Aunt Izzy, as Catherine walked into the kitchen and placed her keys and phone on the work surface. "I've made a pot of tea, would you like a cup, and we could carry on where we left off?" "Yes please," Catherine sighed, slipping her shoes off and stepping into her comfy slippers.

"Right where were we? Now let me think." Aunt Izzy took a deep breath and continued her story, as it was told to her by Janet Kruger over 24 years earlier. Izzy knew she was in for the long haul, and it would take a while to explain all the events of Catherine's early life, that led up to the day of her adoption. Recalling where she had left off earlier, Aunt Izzy started once more to tell Catherine what happened, in the words of Janet Kruger, all those years ago... She began... "Susie had now become pregnant with Todd's child. There was so much animosity between them; Todd wanted nothing to do with Susie, wiped his hands of her in fact, but Susie had tried so very hard to get back into his life, with no success. She was heartbroken, and he free of her. Susie never totally recovered from this love affair; she really thought that he loved her."

"Susie eventually plucked up the courage to tell her parents. As you can imagine Catherine, they were shocked and devastated at the news, but they rallied together and devised, what they thought was a solution to Susie's problem. It was to be their downfall."

"Janet and Mike Kruger weren't particularly well off, and decided to ask the Claytons for help financially towards the baby's upbringing and care. They sent a letter to the Claytons and awaited a reply. This came sooner than expected, but was not the response they were looking for. The Claytons refused to believe that their son would do such a thing, and requested proof. Janet and Mike sat in the kitchen on that dark winter's day, not knowing what to say to each other, wondering what to do next, and angry that they were not believed, but not totally surprised. The only option left to them was to visit the Claytons with Susie, make sure Todd was there and to get Todd to tell the truth; otherwise there would be no help for Susie."

"They arranged a meeting at the Claytons' house for the following week. Both Susie and Todd were to be there and they hoped for a good outcome from this meeting."

"The day finally arrived. The Kruger family sat outside the Clayton's residence for a few moments composing themselves. The house was enormous. Susie had never seen anything quite like it, and the driveway to the house looked long and winding. They were eventually buzzed in through the electric gates and they saw, stretched out in front of them a long tree-lined road that led to the front of the house. The residence could only be described as a mansion. Two tall pillars stood each side of the front door, looming high above the entrance, propping up the canopy that covered the front steps, giving cover to those waiting to be accepted into the huge reception hall."

"Janet rang the doorbell. After a short while, the heavy oak door was opened. Standing in front of them was a maid dressed in a black uniform with a white crisp starched pinafore. "Can I help you," she asked. "We are here to see Mr and Mrs Clayton. We have an appointment," replied Janet Kruger. "One moment please, I will tell them you are here, as she ushered Janet, Mike and Susie into the reception hall."

"Susie could see Todd making his way down the elaborate winding staircase. He ignored her presence and that of her parents, and continued walking straight past them, without a backward glance and into one of the large lounges, either side of the entrance hall."

"Please come this way" the maid ushered, as Janet, Mike and Susie followed her into a large lounge, rather opulent in design, not the Kruger's taste at all, but Susie was amazed at the furnishings, and lavishness of the surroundings. "Mr and Mrs Clayton will be with you shortly. Please make yourselves comfortable, whilst you wait," the maid said."

"Mr and Mrs Clayton entered through the large double doors and into the lounge. "How do you do Mr Kruger?"John Clayton said extending a hand to Mike. Mike returned the favour, and sat down opposite Janet on one of the large gold and black tapestry sofas in readiness of what was to follow."

"I understand that you are under the false impression that my son Todd is the father of your daughter's baby?" "That is correct," replied Mike, "and we are not under any false impression sir, Todd is in fact, the father". "This is absurd. Todd does not lie to us ever. He would have admitted it had it been true, he is a good boy,' replied John Clayton. "Tell them Todd; tell them this is a pack of lies!"

"Todd stood defiantly and denied categorically that he was not the father of Susie's baby. He slumped back down into the chair, as if it was of no importance to him, and was of great annoyance and imposition. "There you are, and there you have it, straight from the horse's mouth, as it were," stated John Clayton, "what more proof do you want?" "Our son would not lie to us," said Barbara Clayton. "You will have to look elsewhere for the father of your baby".

"Mike Kruger was seething with anger. How dare they take the word of that excuse for a son, against the word of our daughter? Susie could see that her father was on the verge of losing his composure, and stepped in stating; "What was that you were smoking when you were waiting for me on the steps of the villa, was it a cigarette or was it a joint Todd?" "Don't be stupid Susie; you know I don't do drugs. Never have. It was a cigarette..." Todd had realised, too late, what he had said, and his mother was fuming! "Todd is this true? Have you lied to us? You have always denied you smoked, so what else have you lied about?" As far as Barbara Clayton was concerned it was only a very small lie, and a very small matter, but nonetheless a lie, and had put doubt in her mind as to the honesty and integrity of her son."

"I believe Todd sat there dear, deflated, unable to retaliate any longer, and eventually he broke down in tears, sobbing like a baby, admitting everything Susie had said was true. Susie had lost the fight but won the battle," Izzy confirmed.

"John and Barbara Clayton excused themselves, leaving the lounge to discuss the matter in private. The anger now agitating deep within his body, John Clayton felt he was losing the control he had developed steadily over the years, to disguise eventualities that he came across in his line of work, and containment he found necessary to get his way in life. "You know that if this ever got out, I would be ruined, not to say what it would do to Todd's future career. We can't take the chance Barbara, we will have to pay them off, for peace of mind, and a little persuasion on our part, to keep them quiet, and to be sure they will never divulge any of this ever to anyone." "Yes I reluctantly agree," Barbara acknowledged, looking straight at Todd for any glimmer of remorse. None was forthcoming.

"Janet told me the Claytons were fuming Catherine, especially Barbara. I believe she said; "If you ever put us in this situation again Todd, we will cut you out of our lives, and you won't be welcome here ever again. Is that quite clear Todd?" Barbara Clayton shouted. "Yes, I'm so sorry mum, I promise it will never happen again," Todd said, clearly shocked by his parents' response, and he promptly made his way up the stairs back to his bedroom, where he stayed for the rest of the evening."

"John and Barbara Clayton agreed to pay the Kruger family a very substantial one-off payment for their silence and the upkeep of the baby in the future. They walked back into the lounge where Janet and Mike were waiting patiently."

"Well I see we have a situation here," John Clayton acknowledged. "I can only apologise on behalf of my son, and any anguish he has caused to you and your family. He will be well reprimanded, but I know that this is of no consequence to you. Therefore I will make a very substantial one-off donation to your family, for the future welfare of Susie and the child, and be assured, there will be no more, and this arrangement, and the circumstances surrounding it, must not, I reiterate, must not, go any further than you and your immediate family. Do I make myself quite clear? Or there will be repercussions." "Are you threatening me John?" Mike replied angrily. John thought long and hard, before answering; "No I am not, but I am warning you, do not cross me or my family, or you will face the consequences."

"John Clayton stood and walked slowly over to the mahogany roll top desk and opened the second drawer down. He took out a large leather-bound folder containing several cheque books. His pen glided across the surface of a cheque, with little hesitation, and signed the bottom right hand corner; John F. Clayton."

"John Clayton handed Janet Kruger a cheque for the sum of $2,000,000."

"Janet sat staring at the figure on the cheque in front of her. "Yes it is a very large amount Mrs Kruger," John confirmed. "This is why I will make this very clear once more; there will be no further correspondence or contact between our two families. Now, is this agreed, and have I made myself absolutely clear? The cheque is post-dated by six months, so please do not try to bank it, as you will lose everything. It must be placed in an off shore account, I would suggest the Cayman Islands, it's a safe haven and not easily traceable." Janet looked over to where Mike and Susie were seated; they had no need to discuss the matter any further, and agreed immediately to the arrangement."

"The journey home for the Kruger's was short, sweet and for the most part, silent. They were still in shock but the excitement was overwhelming for them, they had never dreamt in their wildest dreams that they would ever have this sort of wealth in their lifetime. A safe and secure place was found to hide the cheque until the day arrived when they could safely bank it. Mike immediately opened an off shore account in the Cayman Islands, as suggested by John Clayton, and placed a minimal amount in the account to keep it open until the day came when they could bank the $2,000,000. It couldn't come soon enough for them all"…

Chapter 21
24 Years Earlier

The Blue Note Club was buzzing with students and lecturers, enjoying an early evening drink before heading back to their rooms and dormitories. The atmosphere was heavy with the odour of smoke, alcohol and melancholy jazz music, weaving its way through the club like a soft silk scarf floating in the summer breeze.

Rachael sat next to Danny, sipping her margarita cocktail in their usual corner candle lit table, waiting for Susie to arrive. Susie was late on this occasion, waltzing through the doors looking beautiful in a white cotton smock top and blue jeans, in an effort to conceal any trace of her pregnancy.

"Hi guys," Susie announced. "It's been a while, how are you both?" Before Rachael and Danny had a chance to answer, Susie looked over towards the bar and saw Todd standing there in deep conversation with Brody. "Oh no, Todd's here," she said annoyed. "He is the last person I want to see." Brody cupped his hands and whispered to Todd. Todd turned and saw Susie. He decided to leave, rather than cause a scene, and made his way out of the Blue Note Club, glancing fleetingly over to where they sat and disappeared promptly out of the door. "Thank goodness for that," Susie sighed with relief. The last thing I want is a confrontation with Todd right now."

"Well how are you feeling now that all the worry is behind you Susie?" Rachael asked.

"I feel much happier, after that awful meeting with Todd's parents last week, Susie replied. When I've had the baby I know I can move forward with my life and start afresh here, at the university, for my last year of study." Both Rachael and Danny had discussed Susie's situation on more than one occasion. They were worried that all was not what it seemed. Susie had tried to simplify the situation but she wasn't fully aware, or able or willing, to see the 'full picture'. Things were changing and not for the better. Now it had slowly become clear over the past few weeks that Todd was no longer the happy, confident self-assured person he used to be. He was angry and distant. There was something Susie wasn't telling Rachael, something unsettling and weighing heavy on her mind. She needed to find out what it was, and quickly, before anything unforeseen happened.

The whole family, including Rachael and Danny were there at the train station to wave Susie goodbye. She was on her way to her aunt's in Toronto, to stay for the duration of her pregnancy and to have the baby in Bridgetown Hospital. A room had been reserved for her in the hospital when her time was due. She was seven months pregnant, and growing by the day.

Aunt Sarah was Janet Kruger's older sister. Susie was very fond of her Aunt Sarah, and was grateful to her for taking her into their home whilst she had the baby, and Canada was far enough away to not cause any embarrassment to her family and friends.

Time passed slowly. Susie was now large and very uncomfortable, and she just wanted to give birth as soon as she could. She kept in close contact with her family and Rachael, keeping up with the news and goings on at home and the university. Finally the day arrived. Susie's waters broke. The contractions were now arriving frequently enough to be worrying. She was driven quickly to the hospital by her Uncle Roy with Sarah Kruger in the front seat trying to keep Susie calm, but with little effect. They arrived promptly at the hospital. Susie was helped out of the car by a middle-aged kindly nurse dressed in a blue and white uniform, put into a wheelchair and taken straight to the delivery ward where she was to stay for the next twenty-four hours. She was monitored frequently but she endured a long and painful labour.

The time arrived. Susie gave birth to a beautiful healthy baby girl weighing 7lb 5oz. She was happy but tired. The baby was taken away to the nursery to enable Susie to have a long earned rest. Immediately she fell into a deep peaceful sleep. Susie's mother had travelled to

Toronto earlier that day to be with Susie when she had the baby. Susie was glad her mother was there to give her help and moral support when the time eventually came.

The day had arrived for Susie and her mother to return home to New Haven. Janet Kruger handed her sister a large bouquet of flowers and a cheque for several hundred dollars towards the cost of Susie's stay, which her sister immediately refused and gave back to her. "I don't want any money for Susie's stay Janet, it was a pleasure to have her for this short time, and she is such good company. Please I am glad to have helped you and your family," Aunt Sarah replied. Janet put her arms around her sister, embracing her softly, kissing her on the cheek and thanking her once more for all the help she had given Susie.

Susie stood on the doorstep holding the new addition to their family. "Thank you so much Aunt Sarah, I will never forget your kindness to me and my baby. Please come and visit us sometime. I know it's difficult for you and Uncle Roy, but we will be able to help with the cost of your journey very soon," Susie whispered. Uncle Roy wasn't quite sure what Susie had meant by her last remark, but he didn't question it as Susie, the baby and her mother got into the waiting taxi and waved goodbye. Susie set off with her mother in the knowledge that everything was going to be ok from now on. The taxi dropped them outside the train station for their homeward journey back to New Haven.

***

Susie, her mother and baby Catherine walked through the front door of their house and into the small hallway. It was rather quiet, too quiet in fact, as they made their way down the hall to the lounge to put baby Catherine to sleep in her crib. On opening the door to the lounge, all they could see were colourful banners, pink balloons and flowers, scattered everywhere around the room. The whole family were there to greet them on their return. Susie's brother and sister, back from University and her father Mike, with Rachael and Danny. SURPRISE!! They all shouted together in unison and rushed over

107

to see the new baby Catherine. "She is so beautiful Susie," both her brother and sister agreed, as Mike held Catherine in his arms for just a short while, frightened he may drop her. "Let's have a toast to Catherine," announced Mike: "May you have a long and happy life sweetheart," as they all raise their champagne glasses to toast the new member of the family.

Rachael held Catherine gently in her arms. "She is gorgeous Susie," and as Rachael looked into baby Catherine's eyes, she seemed to smile back at her; she is going to be a good friend to me one day, and a wonderful daughter to you, Susie. This I am sure. Goosebumps tingled on the back of Susie's neck; somehow she knew Catherine was special, as she put her down in her white lace covered crib, to sleep.

Chapter 22
2010

It was late Friday afternoon when John Colbert hastily tidied his desk in readiness for a long awaited lazy weekend spent on his boat. The boat was moored in the Marina Rubicon just one and a half hour's journey from his home in Manhattan. He loved the peace and quiet of the ocean once he was far away from the shore line, and had every intention of playing his music, mainly the Eagles – the band he had followed from a youth – very loudly – as he had favoured in the past.

Most other agents and staff had left for the weekend. John Colbert was always one of the last to leave as a senior member of the team; it was often left to him to secure the office before heading home. There was only one other member of staff remaining – Edna the cleaning lady. She had been with the Agency for as long as John could recall. Edna, as far as John Colbert was concerned, was family. She had got him out of many a problem in the past. What she didn't know about human nature wasn't worth worrying about.

He gathered up his phone and keys from his desk and turned off the brass desk lamp, when his cell rang. He hesitated for a moment not sure whether to let the answering machine take the message or… "John Colbert here," he replied, giving in to the call.

"Hi John; It's Daniel. Sorry to ring you just before the holiday weekend, but any news yet? Haven't heard from you in a while, just thought I'd give you a call to see if anything has surfaced."

"You just caught me Daniel, I was about to leave the office. Look, do you fancy a couple of days break on board *Eleanor* at the Marina, say come over about 8 pm and we can catch up then; if I don't leave now I'm gonna catch all the traffic on the freeway heading home for the holiday weekend."

Eleanor was his much loved Sun Seeker Cruiser he bought whilst still married to Dolores; one of the only things she hadn't managed to acquire from the divorce. He named it after his mother whom he was very close to. She had died in a cycling accident whilst holidaying in the Greek Islands many years before. Although John Colbert came across as a hard and sometimes ruthless character, underneath it all, he could be thoughtful and sensitive. This side of his character he rarely showed to anyone.

"In answer to your question Daniel, yes, I have come across something, a letter that's been kept on file, for a long, long time; I managed to get a copy, don't ask me how, you don't want to know, but again there is something that doesn't add up here. It's marked – 'Code Red – Government Policy Only' – but has only just come to light these past two years."

Daniel knew this was significant. None of it made sense at the moment, but sense of it he would have to make. "OK John, you're on, I'll see you around 8 pm tonight," Daniel replied, as he instantly replaced the receiver and headed straight for the exit.

***

"Night Edna sweetheart," John Colbert called out as he closed his office door. "Oh, goodnight sir, have a good weekend," she replied, and carried on mopping the pale grey marble floor directly in front of John's office. "Mind you don't slip and fall now sir," she said, as he passed gingerly around her and her bucket and out into the lobby, heading straight for one of the waiting lifts that took him quickly down to the front entrance of the Bureau.

John Colbert's time was his own now since his acrimonious divorce seven years earlier. He had one daughter Stephanie by his marriage to Dolores, whom he never saw as she had refused him visitation rights long ago, due to the fact that he had been an alcoholic and a womaniser. He had managed to kick the habit with a lot of help from AA, but because of the numerous affairs he had had in the past, which eventually caught up with him, it hadn't helped his position, and this led to his inevitable demise. He knew he had been a mess, but somehow he managed to turn his life around, although then too late to save his marriage. His ex-wife also blamed the job. This he could not deny.

***

Daniel entered the private elevator that would take him up to his penthouse. The journey was quick and swift, as the doors of the elevator opened out onto the luxurious reception area of the 6th floor of his apartment block. His penthouse comprised of the whole of this floor, far too large for his personal use, but a good investment for the future as far as he was concerned. Walking through the large reception hall in his apartment, he glanced out of his lounge window; it brought back distant memories of the time he had visited the Rockefeller Centre with his girlfriend years ago, and they sat sipping champagne, mesmerised as the dusk met the dawn, both looking southward over Manhattan, it was a spectacular sight, one he would never forget.

Daniel took off his dark grey Armani suit and changed into a casual blue polo sweater and cream slacks – one thing he never denied himself was a wardrobe of good clothes – and what he always referred to as his 'seafaring shoes'. These were in fact navy blue loafers and extremely comfortable; he often wished he could wear them to the bank, but knew that it would not go down well with the Board of Directors, so kept them just for occasions such as this. Packing a few things in his brown leather holdall for his overnight stay on the *Eleanor*, he entered the lift which took him down to the garages below his apartment block and to his black BMW.

Time had been good to Daniel Adams. He looked younger than his forty-two years, with little trace of grey in his thick dark hair. He managed to keep himself fit by working out at the gym every morning at 6.30 am before starting work at the Bank. He had eaten a substantial lunch at the Penza Restaurant in downtown Manhattan earlier in the day, so a meal wasn't essential to him, but a large glass of wine was, after what had turned out to be a gruelling and stressful day at the bank.

Daniel drove out of the underground car park and headed towards the freeway and New Haven. He'd been to the Cruiser *Eleanor* many times over the years, before and after John Colbert's divorce, spending time with him and his family and getting to know John better than most. It was true to say that Daniel liked John Colbert, and trusted him with his life; they had developed a good working and personal relationship over the years that had never faltered.

Ten minutes away from the Marina, Daniel's cell rang. Bluetooth picked up the call. "How far away are you?" asked John. "I've got the Pinot on ice and a Thai takeaway keeping warm in the oven." John never ceased to amaze Daniel, all the years he had known him, and he still had the Pinot and Thai takeaway ready and waiting for his arrival. Predictable but pleasing, he knew him so well. These days John only drank tonic water. Daniel was very proud of his friend. He had never wavered as far as he knew.

"Only about five minutes now, pal. Chill the glass for me, Daniel replied laughing. See you shortly." Daniel drove onto the dock of the Marina, and quickly found a parking space. With a bottle of Chablis and a large bottle of tonic water in a bag in one hand, and his holdall in the other hand, he walked along the Marina to where the *Eleanor* was moored, down the gangplank and onto the deck. John was waiting for him.

John Colbert sat on his white leather wrap round sofa, on the upper deck of the 'Eleanor', caressing a crystal wine glass filled to the brim with tonic water, taking in the early evening sea air. "Daniel!" John exclaimed, as he stood, looking him up and down, "God you look great you bastard! You haven't changed at all" and warmly embraced him, handing Daniel a large glass of chilled Pinot. "It's good to see you Daniel, how long has it been, must be at least a couple of years? Hell we've got a lot of catching up to do, pal." "Yep, and we've got all weekend to do it," Daniel replied. He lightly placed his holdall on the soft white leather seating of the *Eleanor* and sat down, sipping his glass of ice cold Pinot, relaxing for the first time in what seemed forever, staring across the ocean and looking forward to the weekend ahead.

Chapter 23
2010

"Before I continue dear," Aunt Izzy said, looking fondly towards Catherine, "there is something I want to give you. It was your mother's and it found its way back to me many years ago. I think it belongs to you now." Aunt Izzy opened the old floral chest with a small brass key and lifted the lid. She took out a pale pink envelope. Inside the envelope was a locket. Catherine looked at the richly coloured locket Izzy placed on the kitchen table in front of her. It was gold, intricate and oval in shape, with an unusual pearl, ruby and diamond setting. "It's very beautiful isn't it, Catherine?" her aunt declared. Susie never went anywhere without it you know. Mike and Janet bought it for her for her eighteenth birthday. Rachael had one identical."

Aunt Izzy handed Catherine the locket. She sat for several moments with the piece of jewellery in her hands before gently opening the tiny hinge on the side. Inside was a small picture of Susie and Rachael.

"Are you alright dear?" asked Izzy. "You look as if you've seen a ghost!" Still holding the locket with its tiny window open, Catherine showed Aunt Izzy the photograph inside. "This is Rachel with Susie isn't it?" Catherine asked, as she felt shivers travel down her back. Something happened. I know it did, but I'm not sure what. Catherine held the locket tightly in her hands. She saw something... it was over so quickly, she felt the force, the impact. "Look, my hands are shaking Izzy. Whatever happened? There was an accident wasn't there? I know it. Please tell me, I need to know." Catherine sat very still, tears started to flow gently down her face. She had felt something, something beyond her control, but she knew nothing or very little of what had occurred all those years ago. "Oh my dear," said Aunt Izzy. "Please don't upset yourself. Yes you are right, there was an accident, but be patient, let me continue and everything will become clear very soon. I promise."

"As time passed, Susie started to love baby Catherine more and more each day. Janet was a great help to Susie, looking after the baby, and in fact the whole family, including Susie's brother and sister, all helped in one way or the other. It became increasingly clear, that having you adopted was never ever going to happen.

"Susie talked less and less of Todd over the coming months, he became no longer emblematic in her life and she looked forward to returning to university with Rachael and Clara at the end of the summer semester, to take up her life where she had left off.

"The time had come at last to bank the cheque for $2,000,000 that the Krugers had been given almost a year ago. They thought it safe now to do so, and Mike took a week's vacation from work and hired a boat to take them around the Cayman Islands. Teddy and I were great friends with Janet and Mike and we were also their next door neighbours for many years, often taking holidays together, and this trip was no exception. We also hired a small boat and all arrangements had been made for this short holiday break together. We, in fact, booked our holiday arrangements separately, Mike had insisted on this, as he was nervous that we should not be involved and not be seen together until after he and Janet had taken the dinghy ashore to bank the cheque. Mike hadn't trusted John Clayton in any way, shape or form.

"Susie was about to return to university, so Janet and Mike offered to take you with them, on the boat, and we were to follow on, keeping out of sight, all the time, until the cheque was banked.

"Mike had the foresight to write several letters, in the unlikely event that something dreadful would befall them. One was to Susie, another to her brother and sister, one to us, and the other to the CIA. I still have my letter to this day.

"We all set off for the holiday separately, agreeing to meet up once the cheque had been banked. I suppose Mike thought of us as family and he had agreed with the Claytons that only close family would be informed of this arrangement and of the very generous windfall that would eventually come to the Krugers.

"I look back now Catherine, and wonder if Mike and Janet did do the right thing by Susie. Perhaps they should have just let it go, but $2,000,000 was a lot of money then, and also now, I expect they thought it was worth the risk, as I think many would.

"It was a beautiful summer's day, when we set off for the Cayman Islands. Teddy and I took a flight from Boston to Grand Cayman, arriving early afternoon and took a taxi straight to the Marriott Beach Hotel for our weeks' holiday stay. We hired a twenty-three foot cruiser for just one day, just enough time to do what had to be done and cruise around the Cayman Islands before returning to our hotel for the rest of our holiday. Janet and Mike had made similar arrangements, entirely separate to ours of course, in a different hotel, only to meet up when the cheque was firmly deposited in the bank. The following day, Mike phoned Teddy and told him that he had hired a cruiser too, and would be taking it out on the ocean that afternoon. At this stage, we had no idea that they had brought you with them. Mike asked us to look after you, on our cruiser, whilst they took their dinghy ashore and banked the cheque.

"I was rather reluctant to do this, but we had little choice, and as it transpired, it was absolutely the right thing do. I look back now and am, to this day, so thankful that I made that choice.

"We left our hotel after an early lunch. Mike had arranged with Teddy to meet them as far from the shore as possible, around the bay, out of sight of anything or anyone. This we did and we took you on board, for the short time you were to be with us on our cruiser. I remember sitting with you on my lap, and looking out over the ocean. The sea was a beautiful deep turquoise colour, still like a mill pond, the boat rocking gently in the afternoon breeze, and your little face looked up at me with great expectation.

"That was the last time I ever saw Janet and Mike Kruger..."

Chapter 24

24 Years Earlier

The first few months at home with Catherine were difficult and exhausting. Both Susie and her parents were feeling the strain, and although Catherine was a good baby, the constant lack of sleep and crying were an unwelcome jar to Susie's already frayed nerves and before long she became tired and irritable.

The days and weeks flew by and Catherine thrived. Night feeds were a thing of the past, no longer essential and life gradually improved for everyone. Susie was able to establish a daily routine and she began to enjoy Catherine for the first time since returning home from hospital.

Time passed quickly and before long the day arrived for Susie to return to university to continue her studies. Rachael had been there for Susie during the early months after the birth, helping out whenever she could, and loving every moment being with Catherine.

"It's time you started packing Susie," Janet called up to her from the foot of the stairs. "Yes, O.K. mum, I'm just getting everything together now, ready to pack," Susie shouted, as Janet Kruger returned to the kitchen to give Catherine her morning feed. The whole family were in agreement that Susie should return to university as soon as possible to resume her studies and that Janet would give up her part-time job at the school, to take care of Catherine whilst Susie was at university. Susie knew that all financial worries would disappear once the cheque was safe and sound in the account in the Cayman Islands, and there would be no further need, of Janet's small income. The intention was to bank the cheque at the very earliest opportunity.

Susie packed all her belongings that she needed for the new semester at Yale. She was excited, but a little apprehensive, and she couldn't wait to see all her friends again, with the exception of Todd. The thought of bumping into him unnerved her, but she was prepared for any eventuality, and was stronger now, and ready to face him if the need arose.

She walked quickly from the kitchen to the front door. She placed her brown leather suitcase in the hall under the large wooden dresser with its ornate over mantle mirror above. As a child Susie was amazed at the way it reflected the soft sunlight through the small leaded window in the centre of the panelled front door, creating a prism of colour around the hall. It still amazed her.

"Hi Rachael, come in. You will be glad to know I'm ready," as Susie closed the front door behind Rachael. They returned to the kitchen together, where Janet was giving Catherine her morning feed.

"Hello Mrs Kruger. Please can I hold Catherine for a moment?" Rachael asked eagerly. Janet tried to take the bottle from Catherine, with little success! "Let me finish giving her the bottle and then you can have a cuddle Rachael," Janet replied. "She really wants to finish it, she must be hungry. I couldn't be so cruel!" Catherine finished her milk quickly, and after bringing up her wind, Janet stood up and carried Catherine over to where Rachael was sitting. "Hello sweetie, and how's my favourite girl then?" Catherine cooed and chuckled continually looking up at Rachael, oblivious to all around her and everyone else in the room. "She's getting so big Susie, and heavy," Rachael commented, returning Catherine to Janet to have her dipper changed. "I'll change her mum, Susie insisted, I'm going to miss her so much." The tears started to glisten in the corner of Susie's eyes, unable to hold them back any longer; she handed Catherine back to Janet, and ran upstairs to her bedroom. Susie knew it would not be easy leaving Catherine behind, but this hard, she had not anticipated. After a short while Susie wiped away her tears and walked downstairs to the kitchen where everyone was waiting for her. "Are you alright dear?" Janet asked. "Yes mum, really I'm O.K. Let me hold Catherine for a moment then we will have to be on our way." Susie held her in her arms, not wanting to let her go, as Catherine looked up at her with big dark eyes, and smiled sweetly.

After saying their goodbyes and the suitcases stored safely in the trunk of the car, Rachael and Susie head for the university. It was 3 o'clock in the afternoon when they arrived at the halls of residence, having stopped briefly mid-morning, for a light lunch en route. Students were filing past the many notice boards in the main hall, which displayed important information needed for the coming semester. Most of it they knew already and some of it irrelevant and unnecessary jargon, written and posted on identical square white cards, to promote all kinds of work undertaken by students to earn extra money during the coming semester.

Standing behind Susie somebody whispered softly, with an edge of sarcasm; "Wisdom can be found in the most unlikely places." Susie turned slowly around to see Carla standing there. "Carla! It's so good to see you," as she warmly embraced her. "How are you?"

"I'm well Susie, it's great to see you returning to Yale," Carla replied. "I trust all's well with you and the baby." "Yes Catherine is doing really well and getting bigger by the day. Look I have a photo to show you. I know this is the 'boring baby photo syndrome', but just indulge me, and I promise I won't show you again for at least a week!" They laughed and made their way along the now familiar corridor, to their respective dorms.

Walking into the dormitory, Susie noticed the old sepia photograph of the Tuscan villa had been removed. Rachael had had the foresight beforehand to take it off the wall, and replace it with a landscape print. She knew the sight of the picture would bring back bad and unwelcome memories for Susie, so she quickly sneaked into the dorm and replaced the picture whilst Susie was talking to Carla. Rachael's taste in art was unlike Susie's, she liked the Impressionists. Anything out of the ordinary, full of colour and expression; her favourite was Kandinsky.

The following week Janet and Mike Kruger had made arrangements to fly to the Cayman Islands. They had chartered a speed boat for one day, enabling them to travel around the islands and take in a little sightseeing whilst visiting the bank in Grand

Cayman. They then arranged to meet up with their good friends and neighbours Teddy and Izzy, placing Catherine in their care whilst they took the dinghy ashore to deposit the cheque in the bank. No one knew of this arrangement, not even Susie.

Rachael and Susie unpacked their clothes, and on leaving the dorm they met up with Carla and made their way to the Buttery. "I've never seen it so full!" exclaimed Susie. "Gosh we'll be lucky to find a table."

"There's one," exclaimed Susie, "I'll grab it, you get the drinks Rachael."

Susie and Carla made their way quickly over to the far side of the Buttery, and once seated, he was there, three tables away; the one person Susie was hoping not to see that day – Todd. Rachael returned carrying three Cokes on a brown plastic tray, having tried very hard not to spill any. She fought her way through the main body of students lining the entrance to the cafeteria, and noticed straight away, the worried look on Susie's face. "What's wrong," Rachael whispered? "Todd is what's wrong. Is he ever going to forgive me for giving birth to Catherine? I just don't know."

"Look Susie, he was the one who put you in the situation you found yourself in, against your will. It was a very difficult choice you had to make, but you made the right one. I'm proud of you – we all are. Don't ever doubt that. If he can't handle the consequences, that's his problem and his alone to deal with. You are getting on with your life and you have a wonderful daughter now... I will always be here for you – we all will Susie – believe me. You are not on your own." Rachael could see Todd approaching and instantly warned Susie before he reached the table.

Todd and Brody made their way over to where all three girls were seated. "Well, well, well, if it isn't the 'three musketeers,' retorted Todd, sarcastically. You'd better stay out of my way Susie or you might regret it." Todd left and Brody followed close behind after promising to meet up with Carla later that evening in the Blue Note Club.

"Don't you worry about him Susie, Carla and I will make sure he leaves you well alone," Rachael confirmed. They finished their drinks and headed back to the dorms to get ready for an evening at the Club.

Rachael was really looking forward to seeing Danny. She hadn't seen him in quite a while as Catherine had taken priority over everything. She intended to make it up to him that evening.

It was a beautiful late September evening. They had all decided earlier to walk to the Blue Note Club; it wasn't too far, and on such a pleasant evening, they would stroll and take their time, before entering the Club. "Come on Susie," Rachael said growing impatient. Susie had lost her motivation for always being on time since the birth of Catherine, but she was trying really hard get back to her 'old self'. "That dress looks great," Rachael confirmed. "Don't try on any more. Let's go." Susie had already tried on five or six outfits before finally settling on the pale blue dress, with a very short skirt.

Rachael closed the door of the dormitory and locked it behind her. She chose something simple to wear for the evening, but something she hoped Danny would like. A white 'gypsy style blouse', gathered around the neckline and teamed with a tight pair of blue jeans which showed off her figure to its full potential. Her long dark hair fell in folds around her neck showing a simple pair of silver hoop earrings that framed her face and added to the gypsy effect she had hoped to create.

They walked down the corridor to Carla's dorm. "I'm ready girls," Carla announced. "This should be a great evening, let's not let that excuse for a human being spoil it for us. I really don't know why Brody is so friendly with Todd, he's nothing like him, I don't like it, and I've told him so," Carla said. "Todd will end up with few friends." "Yes only the ones he can easily intimidate," Rachael said strongly. "But what 'goes around comes around', he will come unstuck one day, mark my words." Rachael had never liked Todd. Her intuition had never failed her. She knew the very first time she met him, he was trouble.

The Campus was buzzing as they mingled among other students, saying hello to many known to them, as they made their way to the Club.

The tree-lined streets were in their last flush of bloom, allowing the late evening sun to filter through claiming strange angular shadows between the various buildings aligning the route to the Club. The girls passed along the narrow road, laughing and joking before finally reaching their destination.

Clouds were now building steadily overhead in the grey unforgiving sky, as droplets of rain began to fall slowly and heavily.

"Gosh we just made it in time girls." Where did that rain come from," Clara exclaimed. Rachael brushed several raindrops from her forehead that she had not managed to elude, and they all made a quick dash for the entrance to the Blue Note Club.

The sky above the Club did not stay cruel for long. A magnificent rainbow appeared to take away its anger, leaving behind in its wake deep puddles, scattered intermittently on the footpaths and roads all around.

"Here at last," Carla said. "Have we all got our passes?" "Yes I think so," Susie replied eagerly. Rachael took hers from her purse, and gathered all three together in her hand, as they walked through the glass doors to the reception area.

"Hi girls; can I see your passes please?" asked the petite pretty blonde girl behind the counter. "Here you go." Rachael handed over the passes. The young girl stamped all three girls hands with a fluorescent logo, so they could come and go freely during the night and she quickly handed the passes back to Rachael. "Come on let's go and have some fun, and try to forget all that has happened, at least for tonight Susie," Rachael said as they entered through the interior swinging doors and into the thick and noisy atmosphere of the Blue Note Club...

Chapter 25
2010

Josh picked up the phone and dialed Catherine's mobile number. He had wanted to call her before returning to school on Monday to try and arrange a date for the following week.

Catherine and Aunt Izzy were deep in conversation when Catherine's phone rang. "It's Josh from the School Aunt Izzy. I recognise his number. I won't be a moment. Would you put the kettle on and make us a cup of tea? I think we need it don't you?"

Catherine walked from the kitchen out into the hall. The ringing of the phone echoed loudly as Catherine answered the call. "Hello Josh." "Catherine, it's great to hear your voice." "How are you?" Josh replied. "I'm good Josh. What can I do for you?" "Well I was hoping we could have a drink next week and catch up." Catherine replied hesitantly. "That sounds good; how about Wednesday then?" Josh quickly answered. "I'll pick you up about 8pm." "Look forward to it Josh."

Catherine pressed the red button on her mobile phone ending the call and returned to the kitchen, unsure of Josh and his intentions. She wished she had been firmer and said no. Was his interest in her personal, or more of a friendly colleague nature? They had kissed only the once. She had been attracted to him in a strange way, but it had felt wrong somehow and had left a niggling thought at the back of her mind, which kept pressing her for reassurance, but none was forthcoming. She couldn't pinpoint it.

"Is everything ok dear?" Aunt Izzy questioned lightly. "Yes fine, let's have that cup of tea now, eh?" Catherine always made her tea with a teabag in a mug, but Aunt Izzy warmed the teapot before placing the teabags inside. She preferred loose tea, sometimes bringing her own but suffered the tea bags on this occasion – and poured the boiling water immediately over, lid on and covered the teapot with a tea cosy. "You always make a great cup of tea Aunt Izzy, the proper way." "Yes dear, it's so much nicer and more enjoyable, don't you think?"

"Let's continue where we left off Catherine…" Aunt Izzy took off the tea cosy and picked up the teapot, pouring out the tea into two pretty blue and yellow floral bone china tea cups, which Catherine kept just for when her Aunt visited. Aunt Izzy added a little milk and sugar and presented a small plate of ginger biscuits. Catherine listened intently to what her Aunt was about to reveal…

"Now let me see – Ah! Yes… Mike and Janet Kruger were now presumed dead, but the bodies were never recovered. There was an explosion on their boat; it was seen for miles around. There was nothing we could do but watch the horrific sight. I will never forget it as long as I live. I know that Janet would have contacted me somehow if she had survived the explosion. I have never heard from them to this day."

"We stayed behind in the Cayman Islands for several days, whilst the authorities tried to salvage anything from the burnt out and almost completely destroyed cruiser Mike and Janet had hired for the day. Nothing was found. All trace of evidence was destroyed in the explosion, which left very little for the FBI and other authorities to go on, who were involved in the investigation at that time. It was assumed to have been a tragic accident, but why did the FBI have to be involved? Teddy and I were very sceptical and we still had the unopened letter that Janet and Mike had left for us. We knew in our hearts, it was no accident, but we had to get home with you as soon as we could. We did not want you involved in any way, or ourselves. The sooner we returned home the safer we would feel. After so many interviews and liaisons with the American Embassy and the Cayman Island Authorities, we were allowed to return to the USA with you."

"Susie had been contacted and should have returned home the next morning. "I'm not sure she received the message," Izzy explained. She never made it home. There was a terrible road accident. Teddy and I could not believe what fate had handed the Kruger family.

It was the worst moment of my life dear, I will never get over the horrific, and disastrous events that had befallen them."

Catherine sat for a moment, trying to take in all that her aunt had told her in what seemed like hours, but only moments had elapsed for the truth to be finally resurrected from the terrible past that Catherine had to come to terms with.

She was speechless. Choking back the tears, Catherine asked, her hands shaking, "What happened to Susie, Aunt Izzy? What happened to my mother?"

Chapter 26
2010

"This is the nearest thing to heaven, eh John?" Daniel said slowly sipping his ice cold glass of Sauvignon, and looked across the ocean at the late evening sun as it disappeared from the horizon. "Yep, it doesn't get any better than this pal," John replied.

John Colbert refilled their wine glasses, his with tonic water and wine for Daniel. They ate their Thai evening meal, catching up on events, past and present and moments in their memories that had bought both happiness and sorrow to their lives; nonetheless significant. Time passed quickly as they reminisced. "God, Look at the time John, its 1 am! I'm gonna turn in now, we can discuss that important matter in the morning." "OK Dan, sleep well. Good night, pal."

Daniel made his way below, down three steep steps reaching the deck beneath him, and walked to a small cabin at the end of the narrow corridor. He had stayed in this cabin on many occasions and was sure John had expected him to once more.

The cabin was small and compact. A tiny washbasin occupied one corner, with a single bed, conveniently placed at the side of the room, and there were several small windows above that let the moon find its' way through their openings. A small cedar wardrobe stood behind the door allowing enough space for an occasional chair and table to sit well in the far corner, with a silver hurricane lamp resting on its surface.

Dropping his overnight holdall on the floor, Daniel took off his shirt and pants and lay on the bed, and drifted off into a deep and restful sleep. Morning came ahead of time as far as Daniel was concerned. He had had the best night's sleep he could recall in recent days, and could quite easily have slept longer, if not for the sun shining through the windows directly above his bed. He made his way upstairs to the familiar sound and wonderful aroma of cooked bacon that hung heavy on the early morning air, crackling away in a large frying pan. "Wow." "That smells good John. Did you sleep well?" "Yep, like a baby, and you?" "Yeah, must be the sea air; haven't slept so well in years."

It was a beautiful morning, but a slight breeze gave relief to what presumed to be a hot and sultry day ahead. John had laid the small table on the upper deck for breakfast under the white canopy, and they sat and ate their eggs, bacon and toast with fresh squeezed orange juice and coffee.

John had suggested that they take the *Eleanor* out for a spin before getting down to the business of the document John had located. The document had been locked away for years, but now it seemed it had come to light very recently for a specific reason. Daniel couldn't wait any longer. "What was it that was so important about this document John, and its contents, that it was left on file for all those years?" Daniel asked.

"Do you really want to know what I think Daniel? Some of the facts I do know are legit, but a lot of it I am surmising, but in all probability, I think I'm right on the button."

"It appears that a Mr and Mrs Kruger and their daughter Susie, were offered an extremely large amount of money over 23 years ago, in point of fact it was the staggering sum of $2,000,000. I believe this was a sum of money to keep the Kruger's quiet about a situation that came about that would have been highly unfavourable for a certain member of staff at the Whitehouse, if it had leaked out. Did you know any of this Daniel? I have a feeling there is something you're not telling me, Dan. I know that you were at Yale at the same time as the Krugers daughter Susie. Did you know her or anyone who was close to her?"

"Well it was a long time ago now, but I do recall, very clearly that the Krugers daughter – Susie, was pregnant with Todd's child. Todd was a friend of mine, from my university days, I use the term friend loosely, he was an arrogant bastard, we touched base together as a group of friends, but Brody was his closest friend, a lot closer to him than I, and knew him very well. I don't know what happened to Brody; I lost touch with him when I left University. I've never heard from him to this day."

"Fuck, is that right, '$2,000,000?'" That was a hell of a lot of money in those days, I think I might well have been tempted too," Daniel expressed loudly.

"The document I have here is a copy of a letter, Daniel, written and signed by Mr and Mrs Kruger and their daughter Susie. It sets out the terms and conditions by which they received the money and how it was to be banked. It's quite specific in its detail, and I have no doubt, that it is the genuine article. I have yet to get the signatures verified, but I want you to see it first, before I take this any further, because as you know, this should not be in my possession."

Daniel and John sat at the table, under the cover of the white canopy, in the morning sunshine, thankful for the light breeze wafting in their direction, and surrounded by various papers and the all-important document. Daniel sat twisting a pencil continually through his fingers, as John began to read the document out loud.

"It's addressed to: 'WHOM IT MAY CONCERN AT THE CIA,' and signed by Mr and Mrs Kruger and Susie Kruger... only to be opened upon our death."

..."We set out below the circumstances that have led us to the point in our lives in which we find ourselves, and the reasons for the actions that we have taken."

"Our daughter Susie fell pregnant with Todd Clayton's baby, who is the son of John Clayton – the senator. As you can fully understand they did not want any publicity, under any circumstances, and therefore offered us a very substantial amount of money – $2,000,000 for the upkeep of the child. After due consideration, we decided to accept the generous offer, and were asked to bank the sum of money in an off-shore account in the Cayman Islands."

"After giving birth, Susie returned to Yale University, and my wife and I, travelled to the Credit Suisse Bank in the Cayman Islands to deposit the cheque."

"This was an extremely large sum of money. We therefore felt the need to put in writing the circumstances that led to this transaction. Our instincts tell us not to fully trust the Claytons, but in the unlikely event they do not hold up their end of the bargain, you will be reading this letter, and they have probably tried to harm us in some way. Please ensure that our daughter and her baby are well looked after, and our two other children, with the money we have hopefully deposited, and we trust that you are successful in arresting and bringing to justice the Claytons and their son Todd."

Signed *Mr and Mrs Kruger

Signed *Susie Kruger.

***

Daniel was speechless for once in his life. He sat listening to John reading the transcript of the letter from the Krugers. It brought thoughts, long forgotten, flooding back to him; memories that had sat at the back of his mind, too painful to remember, yet happy to lie there in the knowledge that they may one day return.

"There is another document here, Daniel, much more recent. It's from our Head Office, stating that the matter was not acted upon at the time, because of the extreme delicacy of the situation, and that nothing could have been fully proven over 23 years ago. Now there is a good chance of successfully bringing the Claytons and their employees to justice. Apparently it has come to light recently that John Clayton has been making enquiries regarding the $2,000,000 that was deposited all those years ago, which would have accrued quite a substantial amount of interest, and he is trying to track down the account details."

"He knows the cheque was drawn, and transferred immediately out. He couldn't have shown any interest at that time, due to the disappearance of Mike and Janet Kruger. It would have been his downfall. He was prepared to wait, not knowing where the money was transferred to but with today's technology, who knows, it might be possible for him to track the account?"

"We have agents in the field now. It's just a matter of time before we can nail the bastard. I have a feeling that the money is now needed urgently – guess who's running for office Daniel?"…

Chapter 27
24 Years Earlier

The music was loud and vibrating and consumed any conversation the girls may have had. They slowly made their way over to the bar and through the heavily crowded and smoke filled atmosphere of the Blue Note Club. Rachael looked around for Danny but was unable to see him waiting for her at the far end of the bar. Danny hadn't taken his eyes off the entrance to the club since he arrived there. He wanted to see her as soon as she walked through the door. Catching sight of her at last, he immediately pushed his way through students, a mixture of lecturers and local residents out for the evening.

"Hi there guys," Daniel said. "Gosh you all look great tonight!" Daniel didn't wait for a reply. He took Rachael's hand, pulling her close to him, "And you, my sweet, look absolutely ravishing." Putting his arms around her waist, he manoeuvred her to one side, away from Susie and Clara; taking her face in his hands, he kissed her slowly and passionately, not stopping to breath, not wanting to let her go. "I've missed you so much Rachael, don't ever leave me for that length of time again. Promise me?" Rachael was completely taken aback by Daniel's reaction on seeing her again. She was overwhelmed and very happy; life couldn't get any better. "I promise Daniel." They disappeared across the floor, over to the far corner of the club, and began to catch up on the news of the last few months.

The night passed swiftly. Everybody had a great time if a little bit worse for wear as the evening came to an end. Susie had managed to stay out of Todd's way, and Clara spent best part of the evening alone with Brody. Susie danced most of the night flirting with all the good-looking guys she could find, much to the annoyance of Todd. She had consumed way too much alcohol, and found herself unable to stand easily without assistance.

The Blue Note Club emptied steadily. The jazz band played softly in the background, finishing their rendition of 'Stranger on the Shore' as Rachael and Danny walked over to where Susie stood, propped up at the bar, being helped by Clara and Brody, piling her with black coffee, in an attempt to sober her up and get her back to the dormitory.

"I'm going to walk Susie back to the Dorm," Rachael said. "It's not that far. By the time we reach the Halls, she will be sober. I can't take her in like this. They won't take kindly to someone being sick in the corridors. Hopefully she will have been ill before we reach the Dorm."

Daniel tried desperately to persuade Rachael to accept a lift, but she was adamant that if Susie was going to be ill, it would be best in the street and not in Danny's new car. So it was agreed, and Rachael promised to call Danny the next day, to confirm all was well.

Clara got a lift from Todd and Brody, in Todd's car. She was slightly apprehensive, as Todd had had a fair bit to drink himself, but he promised to take it easy, driving slowly back to the Halls.

Rachael helped Susie out of the front doors of the Blue Note Club, down the steps and into the fresh evening air. There were large puddles scattered around the pavements and roads, from the earlier cloud burst they had managed to evade before entering the Club that evening.

Susie stood upright and erect and without warning, ran for the nearest tree. "The last time I was sick Rachael, was in the first three months of my pregnancy with Catherine. I'd forgotten what a ghastly feeling it is to throw up. I'm better now. Thanks for helping me, I really don't know what I would do without you. You really are a true friend."

"I'll always try to help whenever I can Susie, and be with you somehow, you can bank on it." Rachael felt responsible for Susie, she had known her a long time, from a very early age, and was like an older sister to her. They were in fact, the same age. Susie was highly intelligent but immature for her age and Rachael felt she needed day to day help and guidance. She worried about her and what would happen if she wasn't there to pick up the pieces.

Both girls set off on the short walk back to the Dormitory. It had stopped raining, but the pavements and roads were still slippery under foot. Rachael helped Susie along the pavement steering her clear of the puddles.

***

Todd and Brody dropped Clara off at the Halls, and Todd decided to go for a short drive, to clear his head, before turning in for the night.

"Come on Todd," Brody said. "Let's call it a night. I'm bushed." "No, not just yet;" Todd drove down the road, back in the direction he had come.

"Look over there. It's Susie and Rachael," Brody exclaimed. He pointed to the girls walking slowly along the pavement. "Shall we give them a lift?" "Don't be stupid, I wouldn't give that bitch a lift if my life depended on it," Todd growled. "Let's just scare them a little." "No Todd, let's get back to the Dorm." "No, I'm just going to frighten her a bit," Todd replied.

Todd drove chaotically towards Rachael and Susie; he mounted the pavement but didn't allow for the grease on the road and swerved directly into the path of Rachael and Susie. The screech of brakes, applied too late, could not save the girls, tossing them both into the air, so high, so fast and so hard. Their poignant screams could be heard, echoing off the buildings that surrounded them.

"Oh fuck! What have you done Todd? They're not moving. They may be seriously hurt. We've got to go back, NOW! Turn around and go back and call for an ambulance."

"NO! It was an accident Brody. Shut the fuck up and let me think," Todd yelled, as he drove quickly and further and further away from the scene, and the carnage he left behind. "Listen to me. We have got to stick together and we will get through this," shouted Todd. "We don't have a choice Brody."

"You shouldn't have done it man. This is a mistake."

"Look Brody, what's more important, them or us? The two of us – we've big plans. You want a career in law, and I wanna run for Office someday. We both are gonna make a difference in the world. Nobody will know it's us Brody. Don't you see; we don't have a choice. Do you have any idea what will happen if this got out? My dad is loaded. He has lawyers that will cover up all of this, if need be. Nobody saw us, the streets were deserted."

Silence hung heavy in the air as they made their way back to their dormitory. Brody knew, in a macabre way, Todd was right. Their lives would be blighted forever. They didn't have a choice...

***

The sound of sirens could be heard echoing in the early morning darkness. An ambulance pulled away, wasting little time, travelling at top speed, sirens and lights flashing in the still of the night, making their way to the Memorial Hospital, and the Accident and Emergency department, followed close behind by a police escort.

The scene of the accident was now cordoned off and the road closed to all vehicles, except police and medical staff. The Police placed large yellow metal signs, with bold wording, asking for witnesses to please come forward, if they had seen or heard anything of the 'hit and run accident' which had occurred at approximately 1.45 am that morning.

A small crowd of onlookers had gathered at the scene standing around, chatting, wanting to find out what had happened. There did not appear to be any witnesses. Nobody had seen a thing.

The ambulance arrived at the hospital. Susie and Rachael were both rushed through the heavy plastic doors, and were immediately taken to the Intensive Care Unit. Rachael's injuries were so severe, the paramedics had tried so hard to keep her alive until they reached the hospital, but she died in the ambulance, and was pronounced 'dead on arrival'. Susie had sustained severe head injuries and internal bleeding with multiple fractures to her body, and was placed on a life-support machine. She was not expected to survive the night.

***

Todd was dripping with sweat and in a state of panic. He dropped Brody off at the dormitory and made his way home to his parents' house, only thirty minutes' drive away. He drove as slowly as he could so as not raise suspicion. His mind was spinning, but he knew he had to hold it together somehow, and make this work. Turning into the road where his parents lived, he could see their house was all in darkness. "Thank God for that! They're in bed, and didn't go out for the evening," Todd thought to himself. He drove slowly onto the forecourt of the separate garage block, and opened the up and over garage door with his fob. The door slowly raised itself until fully opened. Todd got out of his car and drove his other car, a black jeep, out of the garage and onto the forecourt, then parked his red Mustang in its place.

He knew he would have to tell his parents eventually, as the damage to the near side of his car was visible; dented with the force of hitting the girls, virtually head on, and scraping a tree in an effort to regain control, steering back onto the road. It would have to be repaired immediately so as to leave no trace of evidence of the horrific event that he was responsible for.

Todd knew his father would take care of it, as he had told him in their recent conversation together; "No loose ends next time. Make sure the situation is tidy and finished with son."

Todd was glad he had the foresight to fill the jeep with fuel, the last time he was home. Running out of fuel now would ruin everything, and he wasn't about to let that happen.

Todd drove back to the Campus slowly, keeping a watchful eye for police vehicles on late night patrol, and gave a sigh of relief as he drove into his parking space at the University Campus. He had left the dormitory window open for his return; he didn't want to take a chance on anyone seeing him enter through the front of the building. This was the one time he was glad they had a ground floor dormitory.

He parked the car, and walked silently around to the back of the dormitories. "No one in sight; that's a bit of luck," Todd thought to himself, as he took off his trainers, and climbed through the dormitory window.

Todd was glad Brody was already asleep, as he wasn't in the mood for a heated conversation; he got undressed, fell onto his bed, and into a restless sleep...

Chapter 28
2010

The moment of truth had arrived. It was the truth Aunt Izzy had dreaded giving Catherine since she arrived back in England. Izzy sat uncomfortably in Catherine's favourite armchair, apprehensive as she twisted a white cotton handkerchief nervously in her lap. There was no easy way to tell Catherine what really happened all those years ago. She would just have to be honest, knowing that what she was about to say would not be what Catherine was hoping to hear.

"I'm afraid it's not good news. I'm so sorry dear." Izzy started slowly to relay the truth. Catherine sat listening intently, but fearing the worst. Aunt Izzy stumbled clumsily into the conversation, trying to ease the truth gently to Catherine. There was no easy gentle way.

"It was a tragic 'hit and run' accident that caused the deaths of both Rachael and Susie, as they walked home from The Blue Note Club 24 years ago. The truth is Catherine, Susie was your mother. They never found who was responsible, although there were many theories and speculations as to who caused the accident. It was never proven. At the time, it was thought that the authorities had a good idea who was involved. After lengthy enquiries locally and at Yale University, interviewing hundreds of students, they narrowed it down to about six possible suspects. They were interviewed at length but none were convicted. All had strong alibis and as hard as they tried, no one was arrested for the crime.

"From the information we managed to obtain at the time, Teddy and I had a feeling it was someone who was high in authority, high up in Office, possibly the Whitehouse, but what could we do? We couldn't prove any of it and we couldn't get involved. We had you to think of. We knew that we had to get you away from the Cayman Islands as soon as possible. The people responsible for your grandparents' death would not have hesitated to eliminate you if there were millions of dollars at stake, they would stop at nothing to get their hands on the bank details.

"After many months and years the accident became yesterday's news."

"We made so many enquiries over the years, but to no avail. Dead ends whichever way we turned. It was a tangled tale that had to be unravelled and Teddy and I believed there was a huge cover up that went much deeper. You can bet your bottom dollar, there is someone out there who knows the truth and might now be willing to tell. Maybe one day it will be told. Let's hope so Catherine."

The face before Aunt Izzy could only question why? It was numbness that gripped Catherine first. The deep sorrow and light sobbing followed. "I thought, at last I would know who my birth mother was and where I might find her, but you tell me she died over 23 years ago! This just can't be right Izzy. Everything I've experienced over the last year does not point to that." The tears were now flowing freely down Catherine's face.

Nothing seemed to matter now. The small glimmer of hope Catherine may have had, was now extinguished. "What about the dreams and visions I have had in the past – the Blue Note Jazz Club, the Tuscan villa, the houses; they must mean something and the drawings I drew as a child, what about those Aunt Izzy?"

"I don't know dear, but I know in my heart that this is not the end, but just the beginning for you," Izzy replied.

"I'm going to fly to the States in the half term Izzy and make enquiries, research this deeper. Someone must remember something of what really happened all those years ago, and I intend to get to the bottom of it," Catherine retorted. "It will also give me the opportunity to visit the bank in Manhattan and sort out this account; if indeed the money is mine and if indeed it exists.

"Can I stay with you, it will only be for the week, and it will be company for you. It's been a long time since I visited."

"Yes of course dear, of course you can," Izzy replied. "We had better get the flights booked before I return home then."

***

Returning to school on the Monday morning, Catherine parked her mini in its usual space and headed straight for Martin Castona's office. She had interrupted something the last time she entered his office, which gave her cause for alarm.

"Good morning Catherine, I'm glad you are here; you are just the person I want to see. Please sit down. I'll be with you in just a moment." The Headmaster stood and walked across the wooden floor of his office to the small room next door returning with a large manila envelope. "I have been meaning to give you this since the day you arrived, but somehow never got around to it." Martin Castona handed Catherine the large manila envelope. "The document inside the envelope is pertaining to your future with us here at Braeside School. Please read it carefully. It will help make things seem a lot clearer and it will give you advice on what events you may experience. Read it at your leisure but please do not discuss this document with anyone, especially colleagues in the school. Is that understood Catherine?"

"Yes of course, I understand" Catherine replied, puzzled. "It was given to me in confidence and I was authorised to pass it onto you Catherine," Martin advised.

Catherine's first impression was one of intrigue. "What on earth is inside this envelope that could warrant such secrecy?" Nothing seemed to surprise her any more, and her life seemed no longer her own. She was aware now that obtaining her teaching position at Braeside School was pretty much pre-organised, but by who? Catherine intended to find out, but who could she trust?

***

Catherine left the Headmaster's office and bumped into Natalie Galloway in the corridor. "Hi Catherine, how are you?" Natalie asked warmly.

"I'm good thank you," Catherine said, clutching the manila envelope in one hand and balancing a coffee she had just managed to obtain from the often malfunctioning vending machine, in the other.

"I see you have the envelope that Martin has been waiting to give you. I don't suppose you have had time to read it yet?" Natalie asked in a matter of fact way. "No I've only just received it. I'll look at it later Natalie."

"Gosh there seems to be a great deal of interest in my reading this document. What the hell is in it?" Catherine thought to herself. "I had better put it somewhere safe until I can read it later." Walking slowly down the corridor, deep in thought, drinking her morning coffee she passed the busy and noisy classrooms on either side of the corridor. The walls were adorned with the usual end of term projects and colourful paintings. "Catherine!" Josh shouted out loud. "Wait up!" He peered round the classroom door as the children arrived to take their seats for the morning lessons. "Did you have a good weekend Catherine?" he asked, barely making himself heard above the noise of the children.

"Yes, did you?"

"Not bad," Josh replied. "I'm looking forward to Wednesday. I'll pick you up about eight. Is that OK?"

"Yes, fine Josh, see you then." Catherine could see Josh looking slightly puzzled at the large manila envelope. She was waiting for him to say something. He never did.

There was little time now to find a good safe place for the envelope. Catherine's class was already seated and waiting for her arrival. She entered the classroom. "Good morning children..." "Good morning Miss Morgan," they replied in unison. Catherine sat down, and found the perfect place for the envelope... under the cushion of her chair.

Chapter 29
24 Years Earlier

Todd awoke early the next morning in a cold sweat. He could hear the noisy but muffled commotion in the corridor outside the dormitory. It was 7.30 am.

"Wake up Brody! What's going on out there?" Brody was far from asleep. He rose slowly and sat silently on the edge of the bed with his head in his hands. "What have we done Todd?"

"What do you mean? Don't you go weak on me now Brody, you need to get a grip and keep your mouth shut? Do you understand me?"

Brody sat speechless. He knew full well what they had done and the consequences it held. "Fuck you Todd, you got us into this mess, you get us out of it or I'll go to the cops, I swear I will!"

"Don't you threaten me Brody; I don't like to be threatened. I'll make this go away. Just give me time. Trust me!"

Todd pulled on his pants and t-shirt, staggered slowly across the room to the door of the dormitory, turned the well-worn brass knob and looked down the corridor to see what was happening.

There were crowds of students moving around with no particular purpose and huddled around the news board. Todd moved sheepishly down the hall. He could just make out what was written on the notice board… "If you were in the vicinity of Hillhouse Avenue and Sacham Street last night at approximately 1.45 am and witnessed a 'hit and run' accident, please make yourself known to the Head of Faculty or the Local Police Department as soon as possible." Todd knew he had to stay calm. He also had to tell his parents before they saw the damage to his car and before the news of the accident had fully circulated around the University and reached the local tabloid.

For the first time in his life, he was frightened. He knew all too well what his parents' response would be. They would kill him, unless he manipulated the truth a little. He had no choice.

***

Todd pulled into the driveway of his parents' house. It was 9.30am. He approached the front door, turned his key in the lock and walked straight to the kitchen. John and Barbara Clayton were deep in conversation over coffee and pancakes and looked up to see Todd standing in front of them.

"Hi Todd; you're here early son, didn't expect you till much later." His father picked up the morning paper, and started to peruse the front page and the financial pages as he usually did for as long as Todd could remember.

"Mum, Dad, look I've got something I must tell you. Please don't be mad. It was an accident."

John looked at Barbara and Barbara back at John. The expression on their faces changed to grave concern. They turned very slowly to face Todd.

"What have you been up to now son?" John asked with trepidation, knowing full well it wasn't going to be good. Todd began to relay the events of the previous night, leaving out several major points and turning many important facts to his advantage.

"What the hell were you thinking? Why didn't you just return to the Dormitory like everybody else? Is that it? Is this everything? Is there anything else you haven't told us, anything you've left out?" Todd thought quickly. Should I tell the truth or dig myself deeper and deeper into a web of lies that there would be no return from. He had no choice if he wanted their help.

"OK, OK, I did do it. I ran them down. Is that what you want to hear? But it was an accident, the car skidded and I lost control."

"For a moment I thought you had half a brain in your head. How could you place us in another situation like this; how could you Todd?" His mother shouted at him with anger.

"I'm sorry Mum, Dad," Todd yelled back.

"You're sorry!!!" his father screamed loudly. "It's of no consequence now, what's done is done. You disgust me Todd," retorted his father. "You are a major disappointment to your mother, and I."

Todd was unsure what his parents' intentions would be and started sobbing like a baby. "Pull yourself together son. What we need to do right now is focus. Brody was with you, right?"

"Yes."

"Then the first thing we need to do is call Brody's mother Margaret and make sure Brody says nothing. You both went straight back to the Dormitory after giving Clara a lift, OK? Make the call Barbara, and you had better hope that we can contain this. Now sit down Todd."

Barbara made the call. A long conversation transpired between Margaret and Barbara. Barbara replaced the receiver, announcing – "He won't tell, I'm sure of it John." Todd sat and watched the antique clock's pendulum swaying backwards and forwards as both his parents made various telephone calls, tying all the loose ends, and discreetly arranging for the red Mustang to be repaired by an unnamed person in their employ. There were numerous members of staff on the Clayton payroll of this calibre.

"This is the very last time both your mother and I will be willing to help you. You are on your own after this. Do you understand Todd?"

"Yes Dad – thanks so much; I won't let you down anymore, I promise, I promise."

Todd walked out of the front door, made his way back to the dormitory without a second thought...

Chapter 30
2010

Catherine pulled up outside her house. It was just after 6 pm. Tired after a gruelling day at school, she reached across, picked up her heavy black leather handbag from the front seat and made her way indoors.

Aunt Izzy had the evening meal prepared. Herb roasted chicken and rice, one of Catherine's favourite quick dishes she often prepared for herself after work. She sat at the kitchen table, placing the large manila envelope on its surface.

"What's in the envelope dear?" Aunt Izzy asked.

"I'm not really sure. It was given to me by the Headmaster this morning."

Catherine took off her coat, hung it in the hall and returned to the kitchen. "Open it now dear before we eat, it may be important."

Catherine pulled at the self-sealing envelope until it revealed its contents. Inside was an official-looking document of which the letter heading immediately gave her cause for concern. She read most of the four-page letter out loud. It stated, in so many words that the said "Catherine Morgan" must give up all her rights to the monies deposited 24 years previous in a Swiss Bank Account, as it was, and still remains the right and true property of the US Government and the Office of Mr T. Clayton, who is currently running for President of the United States of America. It continued on in an official capacity to the effect that she should sign and return the attached official slip, with details of the account, sort code and account number. It also stated that if she failed to comply completely with this agreement she would be prosecuted and if found guilty, she could face imprisonment.

"They don't have the authority to do this as the account is now in your name, therefore you are the true holder of the account," Aunt Izzy said angrily. "This document has been sent to frighten you dear; you mustn't let them intimidate you. I have a very good friend in the States who will look at this document for you. He owes me many favours over the years, I'm damn sure he will oblige."Catherine sat puzzled and worried about the letter in front of her. It looked every bit the official document, but was it genuine? "The sooner we get to the States the better to sort this out once and for all," Catherine replied. "I don't like it, it feels wrong, something is looming, I sense it, I don't know what it is, but I think we are about to find out, Aunt Izzy.

"Are you up for this Izzy? It could be dangerous you know." Aunt Izzy looked kindly at Catherine. "There are many ways in which I can help you dear, most of which you are at the moment, completely unaware of. Don't be too ready to pass me over as an old crotchety senior citizen not able to contribute in any way. I will fill you in on the flight back home... but as for now, let's put that document somewhere safe, and retrieve the bank details you so cleverly hid in the bathroom. I know just where to put those details, somewhere they will not be found..."

Aunt Izzy got out her sewing box, twisted it in several directions and lifted out the contents... revealing below a hidden secret compartment...

Chapter 31
2010

Sleep didn't come easy to Catherine that night. Tired and restless, she fell into a fretful slumber... finding herself standing once more on a neatly manicured lawn; there it was again, the large colonial house she had seen in a previous dream. Try as she might, she couldn't make out the name on the large ornate wooden sign directly opposite her. She moved closer and closer until... Catherine shouted out – "I'm inside the house now! I can hear someone faintly calling my name; 'Catherine, Catherine'." She followed the sound up the stairs. "It's dark, I can't see, where are you?" Catherine called out. "Is there anyone there?"

"Catherine I'm here, can't you see me?"

Catherine awoke with a jolt! She tried to gather her thoughts, rubbing her eyes as she tried to focus. "I know that house, I've seen it before but – who was calling my name?"

Catherine fell back on her soft feather pillow into a light sleep, tossing and turning until morning eventually arrived. It was a dark overcast day, not the sort to energise you, but she was fully energised, and she knew exactly what she had to do next. Stepping into her slippers and slipping her dressing gown on, she made her way down the stairs and into the kitchen for a long awaited morning cuppa and switched on the laptop.

It was just after 7 am. Aunt Izzy was still asleep. Catherine hadn't wanted to wake her just yet. The laptop sprung to life, and the kettle had boiled. Catherine made herself a cup of tea and sat down at the kitchen table. "Let's see now." She entered the words: 'Large Colonial Houses' in the vicinity of Yale University or suburbs. "That should do it," she thought. "There are such a lot listed." She hadn't realised there would be so many, in fact far too many to troll through before she left for work. "It's going to have to wait till later. But I will locate this house if it takes me all night," Catherine thought to herself.

Taking a slice of toast and marmalade, Catherine continued upstairs. She heard Aunt Izzy stirring in the spare bedroom. She peeked around the door; "Morning lazy bones, did you sleep well?"

"Yes dear, very well. Did you?"

"No, not really; I had another dream. It was different this time, but I'll tell you later when I'm home from work. The dreams are getting less frequent now but more intense. I know I'm getting closer to the truth, I feel it, but when you get the chance Izzy, could you download all the villas and large Colonial Houses listed in the Yale University area and suburbs? Select the ones that are remotely like the house I described to you and print them off for me, I must find out where the house is located. It's at the heart of this mystery. I have to find it."

Aunt Izzy knew nothing would stop Catherine now, she was so determined to get to the truth, and the truth seemed closer now than ever before.

Making her way down the country lanes to Braeside School, she noticed the grey clouds overhead that hung low. "Mmm... Looks like rain," Catherine thought to herself, pulling into her parking bay. "Only a few days till half term and then USA here I come!! I hope Aunt Izzy has managed to book the flights. This is going to take some unravelling, and some more. But we will find out the truth one way or another. Of this I'm sure," Catherine confirmed to herself.

Chapter 32
24 Years Earlier

It was a bleak, dark morning when Todd returned to the Dormitory from his parents' house.

Brody was nowhere to be found. His clothes and all his belongings were gone. "Where the hell are you Brody? You can't desert me now!" Todd ran from the room, knocking a student over in his rush down the corridor and out into the now heavy morning rain.

He drove straight to Brody's house. Brody's car was in the drive, still warm from the journey, and so too was his mother's Cadillac. "God, this is going to be fun," Todd thought to himself.

He approached the front porch, walked up several steps, to the weathered front door and knocked loudly.

The front door creaked open slowly. Stood in the doorway was Brody's mother. The rain was now lashing heavily against the porch veranda, sending a chair to swing helplessly in its wake.

"Hallo Mrs Myers, is Brody there? Can I come in; I need to speak to him urgently." Mrs Myers glared at Todd with a look of detestation. "I suppose you better had Todd. And by the way I am going to see your mother tomorrow to sort a few things out. Don't make any plans will you?"

Todd wiped his wet shoes vigorously on the porch mat before entering through the front door and into the hall. He had been to Brody's home on many occasions, but this time it was different, very different. Mrs Myers always made Brody and Todd breakfast, pancakes with whipped butter, but not today. The house was quiet except for the chimes of the old antique grandfather clock standing in the corner. Todd walked through the hall and into the kitchen.

Brody was sitting silently at the kitchen table. "Why did you bring your things home Brody? You can't lose it now, you've got to stay calm and carry on as normal," Todd shouted at Brody in a hushed tone, unsure of Brody's mother's whereabouts.

"Todd we've got to go to the cops. It was an accident. They will understand."

"Are you mad?! Of course they won't. Now look here Brody, if you think I am going to stand by and let you go to the cops and ruin our future careers, you're very much mistaken. It can't happen. It won't happen. As time goes by all this will be forgotten and my father and I will look after you in your future career, and your mother's livelihood, you can be sure of that, I promise. So, pull yourself together and bring your stuff back to the Dorm, and we'll go for a few beers."

Brody didn't answer. He sat glaring at Todd. "OK! OK! I will go along with it, but I don't agree with what you are doing, it's totally wrong, and I just hope it doesn't return one day to bite us on the rear.

"Mum! I'm going out. I'll be back later," Brody called out to his mother, and left with Todd and all his belongings to return to the Dormitory.

The weekend came and went without a hitch. The police interviewed most students and teachers who had had any kind of contact with Susie and Rachael. The interview with Todd and Brody was thankfully short and brief, no doubt because of the intervention of John Clayton.

The following weeks passed slowly. The hardest time for Brody was the funerals of both girls. It was a very private affair, with a large number of family members and well-wishers. Mr and Mrs Bryce, Rachael's parents were there, of course, but Mr and Mrs Kruger were not present, pronounced dead after the boating accident in the Cayman Islands. Susie's brother and sister were present, and also Teddy and Izabelle Johnson, the Kruger's very close friends. Danny Adams was there, visibly upset. He was so close to Rachael, everybody thought they would eventually marry, but not now.

Brody found it hard to hold it together. He felt for the families and swore one day he would make it right for them, and tell them the truth, but now was not the time. Nothing could bring them back.

Todd stood at the rear of the congregation, feeling little remorse, and made his way back to the waiting car. "All OK, son?" his father whispered.

"Yes, couldn't be better..."

Chapter 33
2010

"Are you ready yet?" Aunt Izzy asked. "Josh will be here shortly dear. I'm so looking forward to meeting this young man."

It was 7.30 pm Wednesday evening. Aunt Izzy had booked the flights to return to the States for both herself and Catherine – Business Class, as a surprise for Catherine and because she couldn't contemplate the thought of the long flight back in coach! Teddy had left her well provided for, and she received a good pension from her previous job, so why not she thought.

Catherine sat putting the finishing touches to her makeup. She stood and glanced out of the window as a car pulled up outside onto the small paved front drive. She could see Josh sitting in his red sports car, on his mobile phone. Several moments passed. "What's he doing? He's been on that phone now for ages." Catherine picked up her bag and jacket which lay on the floral duvet on her bed and ran downstairs, waiting for the knock on the door.

Aunt Izzy looked at Catherine. "I thought I heard a car pull up outside dear?"

"Yes Josh is on the phone in his car. He's been out there for at least ten minutes!" The phone rang immediately, breaking the questioning silence.

"Hello,"Catherine answered.

"Hi baby, it's Josh. So sorry, I've been on the phone outside in the car all this time. Save me knocking, can you come to the car and we can get going or we'll be late for the restaurant?"

"OK Josh. I'm ready anyway. I'll be out in a moment" Catherine replied, a little put out and a little mystified. "I'm off Izzy. I'll see you later. Don't wait up. I won't be late."

153

Izzy followed Catherine to the front door. "It is a pity I didn't meet Josh isn't it dear, maybe next time?"

It was a pleasant evening with a slight chill in the air. The sun was just setting beyond the bay as Catherine and Josh drove off down the narrow windy cobbled street.

Aunt Izzy was able to get a distant glance at Josh as they drove off. Walking back through the hall to the kitchen, she wondered where she had seen Josh before, or if she had at all. There was something familiar about him, but yet, how could there be? "I'm probably imagining it," she thought to herself, but in her past she had elicited much wisdom, and gained many a skill along the way. Nothing escaped Aunt Izzy.

At 11 pm. Josh pulled up outside the house. "I had a great evening Josh. Thank you for the meal and these wonderful flowers. They are gorgeous."

"I had a great time too Catherine. We will have to do it again very soon."

Catherine opened the car door, stepping out into the fresh evening air, Josh shouted out to her. "By the way, what was in the envelope I saw you with the other day? Have you opened it yet?"

She knew the question would arise sometime during the evening, and it did! She was ready with her answer.

"Oh Yes! Nothing really, just some papers I sent for. They arrived at the school when I first started, but the Headmaster forgot to give them to me."

"Ok; Nothing of importance then?" Josh asked casually.

"No, nothing," Catherine replied. She leaned into the car, giving Josh a peck on the cheek. "I'll see you tomorrow at school, Josh. Thanks again for a great evening."

Josh drove off, and Catherine watched the small red sports car disappear into the distance. "Why is Josh so interested in that envelope?" Catherine murmured to herself walking towards the house.

Catherine turned the key in the front door gently, not wanting to wake her Aunt, and bolted it behind her. She knew she would never have any real feelings for Josh, he just felt like her brother. He was a good friend and that was all.

She climbed the stairs. The house was silent, save for the sound of the crickets heard outside the small bay window in her bedroom. Staring at the drifting clouds passing in front of the full moon, Catherine thought, what a beautiful evening.

Undressing, she slipped on her night gown, pulled the duvet back and climbed into bed. Sinking into the soft down pillow she spoke out loud; "only two days before we go to the States. Finally I am going to find out the truth"…

PART TWO

THE PAST IS PRESENT

Chapter 34
2010

"The end of term at last, and this time tomorrow Izzy and I will be in the USA. I can't wait," Catherine said. She drove from Braeside School back down the country lanes to meet up with Miranda at Colicchio's her favourite Italian restaurant in the harbour. It had been a long time since she had seen Miranda, and it was going to take a long time to explain everything that had gone on in her life during the last month or so.

Catherine could see Miranda's car as she drove into the restaurant car park. It was relatively early in the evening and the car park was quite empty, thankfully she thought, as usually the car park was 'jam packed,' and it was always a problem to park easily.

As she walked through the glass entrance door into the restaurant she spied Miranda in the corner, sipping a large glass of champagne. The waiter showed Catherine to the table. "Would you like a chilled glass of champagne, Mademoiselle?" the waiter asked trying to be cool and trying a little too hard with his fake Italian accent. "Yes, you know, I think I will. Thank you."

The waiter pulled the chair away from the table so Catherine could sit down. It was chivalry at its best, and it always remained one of her favourite restaurants. The restaurant gradually started to fill. Most tables were now occupied as the waiters floated from one to the other, lighting the candles in the old Chianti wine bottles. Catherine loved the way the stems of the bottles were gradually being covered in melted wax that dripped endlessly down, cascading onto the crisp white tablecloths below. "So very Italian she thought to herself."

After the initial hugs and hellos, they settled down, chatting constantly and trying to catch up until the waiter interrupted, bringing Catherine her champagne and the menus for them to study. Before Catherine could speak the waiter interrupted again. "Today's special is… roasted sea bass, cooked slowly in the oven with a light cream and cassis juice. Also we have a special desert – crème brule with ginger jam."

"Sounds wonderful," Miranda replied. "I think I'll have that."

"I shall leave the menus with you for you to decide, Mademoiselles."

Before Catherine could answer, her mobile phone rang. "Hello, Catherine Morgan here." "Hello Miss Morgan, this is Mr Adams from the Credit Suisse Bank in Boston. I do hope you are well, and have received our letter, and have had time to consider the contents."

"It is now imperative that you visit our offices in Boston as soon as possible regarding your account. I cannot discuss this matter over the phone, but if you could give me some idea when it will be possible for you to visit us, I can arrange a suitable appointment."

"Good evening Mr Adams. My aunt and I are in fact travelling tomorrow to the USA. Yes I did receive your letter. There is, of course, much to discuss, as you are no doubt aware. If you could make an appointment for me on Monday, say about 9.30 am, this would suit me fine. I look forward to seeing you then."

"Of course, yes I will and we look forward to meeting you at the Credit Suisse Bank on Monday at 9.30 am. I will email you confirmation and directions to the Bank. Please forward me your email address. Have a safe journey Miss Morgan."

"Thank you and goodbye Mr Adams." Catherine sat initially stunned, but a little excited by the unexpected phone call.

"Who was that?" Miranda asked. "That was the CEO at the Credit Suisse Bank in Boston where this account is held. I'm meeting him Monday morning at 9.30."

"This is where it really begins Miranda. The truth - and the whole story at last. I'm going to find out what really happened all those years ago…"

Chapter 35
2010

"Here at last Izzy. Have you got your passport ready? We'll be at the front of the queue before you know it."

"Yes dear. Do stop fussing. I know I'm a little ancient, but believe me, I am still in control."

"Yes I know Izzy, you are more in control than I am, that's for sure," Catherine said, stifling a little giggle.

Moving closer to the front of the queue, Izzy could feel eyes burning into the back of her head. She turned around very slowly, to see a man in a scruffy blue anorak and dark glasses staring directly at them. She noticed him earlier, and she had an uneasy feeling about him then, a feeling she had experienced many times before in her life. He looked conspicuous in an inconspicuous way, as he tried to blend into the crowds of passengers queuing, but failing miserably. Izzy knew an undercover agent when she saw one.

"Are you travelling with us today for holiday or business Miss Morgan?" the ground hostess asked on the checking in desk of American Airlines. She was well turned out, as were most of the ground crew working alongside her. Her long brown hair was tied neatly behind in a pony tail, she had very little makeup and perfectly manicured nails. "Holiday, I'm staying with my Aunt for ten days," Catherine replied.

"That's quite in order then Miss Morgan, do have a nice holiday," the hostess replied, handing Catherine's passport and documents back to her. Izzy handed over her documents and passport to the hostess. Checking in for Izzy was a lot quicker and less bother, being a citizen of the United States, fewer formalities were required and the staff member quickly handed Izzy's passport and documents back to her. "Have a nice holiday Izzy," she said, smiling widely at her. "Thank you dear. That's kind of you, if a little cheeky." Izzy laughed to herself and they both made their way to Departures.

"This was such a wonderful surprise – Club Class, Wow!! I've never travelled in Club before; this is going to be great! Thank you Izzy."

"It's my pleasure dear, now let's have a drink. I think we need a glass of champagne; no, let's have a glass of Bucks Fizz with our breakfast? What do you say Catherine?"

"Sounds good to me Izzy," Catherine replied excitedly. They settled down in their seats, fastened their seatbelts and waited for the plane to take off and the long awaited breakfast to be served.

Izzy had seen the man with the dark glasses she had noticed earlier, boarding the plane. He was seated in coach. She decided not to worry Catherine at this time and would wait to see if anything developed during the flight, or if it was perhaps just her imagination. Izzy was very rarely wrong. She had had expert training, and this part of her life she was just about to divulge to Catherine.

The plane sped along the grey tarmac of the runway and rose steadily, sweeping up through the white scattered clouds, into the blueness beyond. It was a reasonably calm day and the likelihood of turbulence was minimal. The plane levelled and regained a steady speed as the cabin crew busied themselves preparing breakfast for the passengers and handing out the daily newspaper of their choice.

"Would you like coffee or tea with your breakfast Madam," enquired the pretty oriental stewardess. "Oh, eh coffee please and could we have two glasses of Bucks Fizz with that?" replied Izzy. "Of course Madame;" breakfast won't be long we are just preparing it now."

Catherine sat back in her seat, relaxing for the first time in several weeks. "I could get used to this," she exclaimed, as Aunt Izzy handed her the breakfast and the Bucks Fizz. "Croissants and fresh fruit, coffee and a Bucks Fizz what more could you ask for?" Catherine thought, enjoying every moment.

"Catherine, there is something I have been meaning to tell you for some time now. It's important that you listen and appreciate what I am about to tell you. It will help you understand more clearly everything that has happened to you in the past and what is yet to come."

"What is it Izzy?" Catherine replied, eagerly waiting for what Izzy was about to say.

"As you were aware, Teddy and I had very important jobs during and after the war. That was one of the reasons we travelled so much and never had any children of our own. There never seemed time, or it was never the right time. I was a code breaker for the War Office and later for the CIA and Teddy was a high-ranking Agent for the CIA. That is how I met Teddy. We were in fact undercover spies for the American government...

Chapter 36
2010

Catherine slumped back in the large leather airline seat, taking a moment to digest everything that Izzy had just told her.

"Are you saying that you and Teddy were spies?" Catherine laughed out loud. She wasn't sure what she was supposed to believe. "No, No I don't believe you, I would have known after all these years; you would have given something away Izzy, you can't hide something like that for such a long time; I would have guessed," Catherine said, shocked and amazed at Izzy's revelation.

"No dear, we were very, very careful and well trained in the art of hiding secrets; we had plenty of practice you know.

"There is something else Catherine, please don't be too shocked, they would not have wanted to upset you – your mother and father were also involved in espionage – they worked for MI5; they were also agents, highly acclaimed and much respected, and like Teddy and I, were in danger most of the time. It came with the territory that one day your luck might run out. But they made sure you were kept safe all of the time to the best of their ability."

"Years ago they wanted to start a family. They were considerably younger than us and had indicated their desire to adopt a baby, so when the opportunity arose, and we realised you were in grave danger when your grandparents were eliminated, we took a risk, made a decision, and took you to safety. Yes your adopted parents were also eliminated Catherine. There was no doubt of that. It was no accident."

"Going back to the Cayman Islands all those years ago, we had to act quickly to get you away from there, before it became feasible that you may not have been on board that yacht at all."

"By the time we got you out of the Cayman Islands and back to the USA, we were told of the death of both your real mother and her close friend Rachael. It was a truly difficult time dear, but we had a great deal of help from our colleagues in the Agency. It was touch and go whether we would pull it off. But we did."

"I am sure you now believe the worst regarding your adopted parents' deaths, and you would be correct in assuming they were assassinated, they knew too much, much too much, of which I have little idea. They assumed it would be safer for both of us, not to have this knowledge. What they knew must have been top secret and highly dangerous as we always confided in each other's activities; I need to find out why they were killed, and I intend to Catherine. They were very dear to us."

"To this day, I am certain nobody knows who you are, only that Catherine Morgan is the sole beneficiary of the bank account in the Credit Suisse Bank in Boston."

"We have a lot of digging to do when we reach the USA; I hope we don't run into any trouble, or I will have to call in a few favours from friends. Yes, that is what I shall do if need be."

"Izzy, this is like something out of a James Bond movie! You've made this up, haven't you? Tell me you have."

"No, no dear, I haven't, it is all completely true, unbelievable as it may seem, but I am sorry to say, true."

"My poor mum and dad. I had no idea. They were really brave, weren't they Izzy? I want more than anything now to find out who was responsible for their deaths and the death of my birth mother and her friend Rachael. But who and where is my birth father now Izzy? I am sure he must be involved somehow, and why hasn't he come forward? We've got a lot of work to do, and the first place we will go to once in the USA, will be the Credit Suisse Bank in Boston..."

Chapter 37
2010

When Izzy and Catherine had finished their breakfast, Izzy closed her eyes. Moments later she was sound asleep. A tall good looking blonde-haired steward covered Izzy gently with a thin soft blanket as she snuggled into the small pillow supplied by the airline.

Catherine always opted for a window seat on a flight. She liked looking out at the white clouds below. When she was a child her mother would tell her that she would point to the clouds and say that they looked like 'little balls of cotton wool'. This was still true to this day, glancing out of the window, they seemed to float on a sea of deep blue sky extending as far as the eye could see.

Catherine felt her eyelids getting heavier until she could no longer fight the tiredness and gave into a welcome sleep... very quickly she was able to establish that this was no ordinary dream she was having. As previously she could see people and places, but not through somebody else's eyes this time, it was different. She could see snatches of a time line from the past. She found herself standing in a dimly lit alleyway. Night time – dark except for the full moon shining down lighting the open doorway of what looked like a lock-up garage. She saw three, maybe four men dressed in grey overalls, wiping their greasy hands on dark stained oil rags and moving quickly and meaningfully around a car covered in sheets. Catherine moved closer to see inside. The car, possibly a Mustang she thought, not that she knew much about American cars, was covered in masking sheets and was having a fender sprayed. "I can make out the old large battered clock on the wall of the garage," Catherine thought. "I think it says; yes it's 1.35? It must be early morning. But who gets a car sprayed at

1.35 in the morning?" The phone that was resting precariously on the arm of an old leather armchair which had seen better days rang loudly, nearly sending it hurtling downwards to the floor.

One of the mechanics, he seemed to be the one in charge, answered the phone. "Hello sir, yes we're nearly done here, you can have the car back in a few hours. Don't worry, no one will ever know it was involved in a road accident, it's as good as new..."

Catherine woke with a jolt. "That's why they never ever found the vehicle involved in the 'hit and run'. It must have been re-sprayed within 24 hours of the accident, all tracks covered. No one ever suspected. Why would they? And why did they not check vehicles in the area and the university? Maybe they didn't have the forensic knowledge they have today, or was this a cover up from the start?" Catherine thought to herself.

"Would you like coffee Madam?" asked the stewardess as Catherine rubbed her eyes, trying hard to focus. "Yes, thank you." The stewardess poured the filter coffee into a white china mug and handed it to Catherine as she sat back in her seat trying once more, to fit all the pieces of the puzzle together. The truth was starting to unfold, but still there was so much that didn't make sense. "I've got just two weeks to find out the truth, with the help of Aunt Izzy – I'm sure it won't be a problem for her." Catherine laughed to herself, still not quite sure what to believe. Had Izzy really been an agent for the CIA in a previous life?

Catherine finished her coffee, sat back and drifted off to sleep once more...

Chapter 38
2010

"Wake up Catherine," Izzy whispered as she gently stroked Catherine's arm. "We are about to land dear." Izzy fastened her seatbelt whilst the cabin crew busied themselves in readiness for landing.

Still half asleep, Catherine stretched her arm up to alter the air control on the panel above her head. It was far too cool now and she placed her cardigan around her shoulders for extra warmth. The stewardess made her usual journey down the centre aisle making sure everyone had their seatbelts fastened for landing, and spoke across Izzy to Catherine. "Please fasten your seatbelt madam. We will be landing shortly. Thank you." Catherine fastened her seatbelt and sat back in her seat. She felt excited and slightly nervous at the prospect ahead of her, and sensed the danger that may not be far away. For the first time in her life, she felt anxious.

She began to feel the aircraft sway from side to side, slicing through the light turbulence, landing with a considerable thud, as it reversed its engines to slow its speed on the approach to its allocated parking bay.

Catherine unlocked her seatbelt. Izzy stood up and located their luggage in the above locker, and they waited patiently for the usual announcement to be relayed across the speaker system... "Please do not switch on any electrical devices until you are well and truly in the terminal building and please make sure you have all your personal belongings before leaving the cabin. On behalf of Captain James and his crew, we hope you have enjoyed the flight today with United Airlines and wish you a safe onward journey. Have a nice day."

"Have you got everything Izzy?"

"I think so dear, I just need my glasses. Now where did I put them?"

"They're on your head Izzy," Catherine replied giggling.

"Oh dear I will forget my head one of these days."

Moving towards the front of the cabin, Catherine caught a glimpse, out of the corner of her eye, of a man in a hurry, almost running, pushing past people in the next aisle to reach the front, as he made his swift exit.

"You looked as if you recognised that man with the dark glasses Catherine?" Aunt Izzy enquired.

"Well, I'm not really sure, I thought I did. He had an uncanny resemblance to someone I know. It couldn't possibly be him, he would have told me. Anyway he is off on some trekking holiday in the Cotswolds."

The stranger in the blue anorak had long gone by the time they reached passport control. The Customs procedure was pretty well straightforward as they exited the terminal building and made their way out to the taxi ranks of Boston Airport.

Izzy grabbed the first empty cab she could find and they headed home to her house. Catherine was now unsure and confused. "Was that Martin Castona she saw hurrying away…? No, it couldn't have been, could it?"

The cab driver was of Mexican origin. He was about 45 years of age, had a rather pleasant face, olive skin with soft dark brown eyes, and a dark moustache that drooped down each side of his mouth. "He just needs his sombrero and poncho and he could easily be comfortable as an extra in an old Clint Eastwood movie," Aunt Izzy remarked. "Yes, you're right," Catherine laughed to herself.

The taxi pulled up outside Izzy's house. They got out of the cab and the driver helped them both with their luggage. Catherine paid him and bid him adios and he was gone.

"The house; it's just the same as I remember it Izzy," Catherine announced. "It has the same grey and white veranda, needing a little TLC now, but charming just the same, and the wind chimes, moving in the breeze, so clear in my memory."

They approached the front door. Aunt Izzy placed the key in the lock, and walked inside. "Let's have a nice cup of tea dear, there's a lot to discuss, but it may have to wait till the morning, I am a little tired."

Catherine carried the cases through the hall to the kitchen, and Izzy placed her small needlework box on the table. "This must be kept somewhere very safe. It cannot get into the wrong hands," Izzy said as she opened the larder door, and walked inside. Moving a large bag of flour and two jars of cooking sauces, she pressed a panel, which immediately slid across. She placed the needlework box inside the empty space and pressed the panel again to close it. She put the flour and sauces back in their place, and closed the pantry door behind her. "Now I am sure it will be safe in there dear."

Catherine stood with her mouth open. "You were telling the truth then about you and Teddy being agents. It's amazing that you were able to keep this to yourselves all these years. I had no idea! None whatsoever!! I didn't actually believe you," Catherine confessed.

"Yes dear, I was telling the truth, and perhaps you will believe me now when I say that we could be in grave danger if we are not careful. You must listen to me and heed what I say. It is very important. Do you understand Catherine? These people are ruthless and will stop at nothing. We have to tread carefully and slowly."

Catherine stood dumbfounded. "Yes I think now I do," she replied. Shivers ran up and down her spine. What have we got ourselves into? It's too late now to turn back, and I must know the truth finally. Someone or something is urging me on, and just for that reason alone, I know the truth is out there somewhere and I am going to find it!

Aunt Izzy put the kettle on as Catherine stood in front of the window. She looked over the misty lake and beyond, remembering the lazy summer days and the many happy holidays spent there as a child. Izzy put her arm around Catherine's shoulder. They sat down and had a cup of tea from Izzy's bone china tea service, quietly contemplating and both wondering what now lay ahead for them...

Chapter 39
2010

Monday arrived like any other Monday. The exception being it was the day of Catherine's meeting with Mr Adams, the CEO at the Credit Suisse Bank in downtown Boston.

Aunt Izzy was already washed and dressed in her usual attire. She chose a multicoloured, full-length floral cotton dress, which she wore with several rows of similar coloured beads, and of course, her trademark trainers. She was eccentric to the point of being a little bohemian, but Catherine loved her for it. She had breakfast already laid out on the kitchen table and the bank details tucked safely away in her handbag.

They finished their eggs, toast and coffee, cleared away the dishes and headed out of the front door, making their way to downtown Boston in Izzy's small blue VW Beetle. Izzy's car had definitely seen better days. There were numerous rust spots and dents to its bodywork and part of the back bumper had been missing, as far back as Izzy could remember. Izzy's usual comment was, "It all adds to its character. This car has seen me through many an awkward situation dear. Yes 'Bessie' is a loyal and reliable friend. "I shall miss her when she finally retires." "I have no doubt of that, she certainly has many, many miles on the clock," Catherine jested. Catherine watched the speedometer quickly approach 80 mph. "Wow, shall we slow down a little Izzy, we want to get there in one piece, don't we?"

"Do you know Izzy, last night I researched the Credit Suisse Bank and found a great deal of information on them. They certainly have some past history to live up to. Listen to this. 'The Credit Suisse Bank' in Federal Street in 1978 was bought by Merrill Lynch and partnered with First Boston. It became Credit Suisse First Boston. There were many deals made, one being the "Burning Bed" deal in 1988 for a loan of $487 million to Gilban and Green for the purchase of a child mattress company, purchased at 20 times its annual revenue.' There was also a purchase of $475 million for junk bonds. The market crashed. Gilban and Green couldn't pay. Credit Suisse injected $725 million to keep First Boston in business which led to it being taken over by Credit Suisse."

"They survived the Wall Street financial crisis, but were investigated into the use of A/Cs for tax evasion; part of a large crackdown in Brazil apparently. Credit Suisse cut 2000 jobs in response to a weaker than expected recovery."

"They seem to have made a pretty good recovery now; we are just about to have a meeting with the CEO of the Boston Branch to finalise a rather large amount of money that I think I am about to inherit. It doesn't seem real, does it Izzy, but by all accounts it may well be. We'll find out one way or the other in a short while. The two hour journey passed quickly as they turned left into Federal Street and headed straight."

Turning left into Federal Street, Catherine and Izzy headed straight for the undercover car park of the Bank.

***

John Colbert arrived a little late for his early morning meeting. He approached the heavy double glass entrance doors to Daniel Adams office. He knew what he had just done was highly illegal and could lose him and Daniel their livelihoods. As far as he was concerned there was no other choice, or they could let the dubious characters in the employ of Todd Clayton... get their hands on the bank details they had been trying to obtain for the last year.

"Good morning Mr Colbert. Mr Adams is expecting you, please go straight through." John Colbert walked past Daniel Adams pretty and efficient secretary, blowing a kiss as he passed, and into an inner lobby knocking briefly on the door marked: Daniel Adams – CEO. He hesitated at the door for a moment, thinking back to how much Daniel had achieved in such a short time. John Colbert was proud of Daniel and proud to be his friend.

"Morning Dan; How are things progressing?"

"Not bad John," Daniel replied.

"Have you got all the paperwork we need?"

"Yes, it's pretty straightforward. The guy owed me 'big time,' he certainly paid me in full and more on this one."

"We'll have to make it quick, Catherine Morgan and her aunt will be here in 30 minutes. What have you got, and did the transfer go through?" Danny asked anxiously.

John Colbert sat down in the Barcelona brown leather chair in front of Daniel's desk and proceeded to take out the documents from his well-worn leather briefcase. "This briefcase has seen a lot of deals over the years, not to mention a few bullets, eh Dan?"

Daniel Adams looked at John as a slight wry smile breached his face. "Yeah, we've had a few moments, eh John?" John read the transcript of the transfer. "It's completely untraceable, as you asked. My source used a ripple exchange to have frat currency converted to e. cash and then into bit coin. He ran the whole transaction through a graphic extension at the protocol level and then through a two-tier laundry service, which he knew he could trust. I would stake my life on his genius, he is the best Dan."

"Well let's hope so John, you've never let me down yet. I trust you," Danny replied. "Great job mate, I owe you one. Now you had better get out of here, Catherine and her aunt will be here any moment."

***

"Wow," he has certainly done well for himself Catherine. A far cry from his days at Yale University," Izzy commented.

"Do you know of Mr Adams Izzy?" Catherine asked.

"Well I do know that he was at Yale the same time as your mother and her friend, Rachael, but that is all I know."

Daniel Adams' secretary ushered them through the spacious reception hall. "Yes he is expecting you Miss Morgan. Please walk through the inner lobby and take the second door on the left."

The brass plaque on the door in front of Catherine, bearing

Daniel Adams' name, gleamed as the sun shone directly on it through the small open window at the end of the hallway. Catherine knocked gently on the door. "Come in," Daniel replied. Catherine and Izzy entered Daniel Adams office...

Chapter 40
2010

"What do you mean, it's disappeared?" shouted Todd Clayton. "My sources informed me only yesterday that it was still in the Cayman Islands. What's happened to it? Where is it now? No one can access that account without prior knowledge of its passwords and security information. I know I've been trying for fucking years!

"I want that money found before Catherine Morgan is able to access it. That money is mine, I need it to fund my election campaign and there is no way she is getting her hands on it, believe me!!

"Find that fucking account Brody or get hold of Catherine Morgan and bring her to me and I'll get the information out of her one way or another. Do you understand me Brody?"

"OK!! OK!! Todd." Brody Myers could see Todd's face contorting in a way he had never seen before, eclipsing any past temper tantrums he had had, and there had been many of those to take into consideration. He had become more like his father over recent years, and in the past Brody was prepared to make excuses for him, but no more. Enough was enough. "How could this man become the President of the United States, FFS" Brody thought to himself.

Brody reflected how on earth he ended up working for Todd all those years ago. But did he ever have a choice? What had occurred on the night of the accident was irreproachable, and irreversible, and he would never forgive himself for not coming forward at the time. But as time went on, it just seemed to have been left behind and life went on.

Todd had secured Brody's future by placing him on his staff, giving him a huge salary and all the trimmings that went with it, cementing his loyalty to Todd. Brody was grateful for that but loyalty would only stretch so far. He had done things for Todd that he was not proud of and would always regret, but this would now have to stop, whatever the circumstances.

Brody was about to take a big risk, he had thought about this day for a long time, it had finally arrived – sitting on the edge of his office desk, he glanced at the photograph of his wife and children, looking back at him in the ivory-coloured picture frame. He took a deep breath. I can't do this anymore – fuck Todd Clayton!!

Chapter 41
2010

Daniel Adams quickly opened the large sealed brown envelope in front of him. It was obvious that John Colbert had not had time to investigate the contents before rushing it over to him. The seal had not been breached and the inner contents were still tightly enclosed in a plastic cover.

Daniel opened the sealed plastic folder and began to read swiftly the front cover of the document. "This isn't right." He quickly scanned the front page again. "As far as the bank is aware, no one has access to this account except the Krugers and they are deceased! It seems that someone has. It appears they have been successfully accessing it over the last 20-odd years, and on more than one occasion."

The knock on the door jolted Daniel into action as he quickly made ready for Catherine and Izzy's morning appointment, tidying his desk and putting out of eye shot the document he had looked at briefly.

"Come in," Daniel called softly. Catherine and Aunt Izzy entered the office. "Good morning Miss Morgan, please take a seat," Daniel said, quickly shuffling papers and organising his desk once more.

Catherine hesitated, glancing over at Izzy. "Good morning Mr Adams;"as they both shook hands with Daniel. "It's very nice to meet you at last. May I introduce my Aunt Izabelle Johnson; do you know of my aunt, Mr Adams?"

"Well, I have heard many stories about you Izabelle," replied Daniel enthusiastically. "It seems you have quite a reputation in certain circles, but I'm not sure these stories are all trustworthy. It appears Izabelle has a rather famous, or should I say infamous, past to live up to."

"Well, Good Morning Mr Adams. I didn't realise I had such a reputation that went before me," Aunt Izzy replied. "Now there's a thing, wouldn't Teddy have been proud of me?" Catherine wondered how on earth Daniel Adams knew of Izzy. She was just beginning to realise how important Izzy was, or possibly still is?

"Please take a seat and I'll be with you in a moment. I have a few last minute alterations to take care of. Would you like coffee or maybe some tea?" Daniel asked. Catherine looked over at Izzy, as they both agreed coffee, white with no sugar would be agreeable.

Daniel picked up the phone, and spoke briefly to his secretary, ordering the morning coffee for Catherine and Izzy. "I won't be long. Please make yourselves comfortable." Daniel left the office and made his way to an outside office where he wouldn't be disturbed.

"God, Izzy!! I'm so nervous!! What am I doing here? This time last year I was just a student teacher looking for work. I can't believe this is happening to me."

Izzy glanced over at Catherine and could see the strain on her face for the first time since they arrived back in the States. It was beginning to take its toll, and she was worried for her safety and well-being. Izzy knew the danger now facing her and she was prepared to do all in her power to look out for her. "Don't worry dear, I'm here now and I will pull out all the stops to protect you."

"Thank you Izzy, that's a relief, I thought you'd given up on all that spying stuff. I really don't know what I would have done without you," Catherine replied.

A gentle knock on the door brought Catherine and Izzy back to reality. The office door opened and Daniel's secretary entered. She was a pretty girl and wore a blue fine knit sweater dress that clung to her curves and on her feet were classic low heeled shoes that matched perfectly with her outfit. Her hair was blonde, short and neat and she wore brown tortoise shell glasses that gave her a possibly undeserved studious appeal.

"Coffee and biscuits, Miss Morgan," she announced. "Enjoy." Placing the tray solidly on the side table, she left closing the door quietly behind her.

Catherine took her time and slowly plunged the caffitiere down into its glass container until all the coffee was immersed. Waiting a few moments she poured Izzy and herself a cup of dark aromatic coffee, adding milk into the white bone-china cups.

Taking several sips of coffee, Catherine relaxed back in the soft leather armchair before noticing the silver picture frame sitting to the side of Daniel Adams' desk. She could only see a small part of the photograph from where she was sitting. Placing her cup on the coaster provided, she gingerly reached across the desk, turning the picture frame around towards her.

The photograph was of a young woman who could not have been more than 18 years of age when it was taken. She had long dark hair that seemed to blow gently in the breeze. She possessed a rare beauty that was not unfamiliar to Catherine and yet the photograph, surely taken on a beach as she could just make out the surf of the sea in the distant background, was not known to Catherine. The photograph was considerably old, but the happiness of this girl still shone from her face. Catherine wondered if she would ever be that happy.

On closer inspection of the print, Catherine froze! Goosebumps raged up and down her spine. The girl in the picture had around her neck, something very familiar to Catherine – a necklace. It looked identical to that of the necklace given to her by her parents. How could this be? What does it mean? And more to the point what was this photograph of this beautiful young woman with the necklace, doing on Daniel Adams' desk?

"Catherine. What's the matter dear? You look as if you've seen a ghost," Aunt Izzy asked.

Chapter 42
2010

Brody picked up the secure phone and dialled a local number. It rang several times before it was answered. "Hi Buddy, how you doing?" "Good" was the reply. "Can you talk?" "Yes I'm on the secure line," replied Brody. "Go ahead."

"It's on, and it's gonna be tomorrow, do you understand?" "Yes I'll be ready," Brody replied. "Good, we can't afford any mistakes at this stage." "Don't worry I'll get him there. 2.30 pm at the chosen rendezvous." "Bye Buddy, see you tomorrow, and good luck" was the reply. Brody quickly ended the call. He knew the risk he was taking, not only with his life but his family would also be at risk. These people were ruthless. How on earth did he ever get mixed up in this world?

"Too late to ponder now," Brody thought, "get on with the task in hand and stop this madness once and for all." Contemplating his next move, he picked up the photograph of his family and held it tight in his hands.

Chapter 43
2010

Daniel walked hurriedly back to his office. Time was now of the essence. He had to speed this transaction through as soon as he possibly could. The money was safe – well hidden. Only he and John Colbert knew of its new existence, its new safe haven – the account numbers, pass codes and location, carefully hidden away.

"I'm sorry to have kept you waiting Miss Morgan." Daniel quickly sat down and swivelled his chair around to face Catherine. "Now I'm sure you have many questions to ask me, but before we start, could you please give me your identification papers, passport and of course the important documentation regarding the deposit account in question. I cannot proceed any further until these have been verified."

Izzy stood up, took out of her bag the documentation requested, and handed it to Daniel. "I have the code numbers you requested to verify the account," Aunt Izzy confirmed. "They are safe. Trust me. I will let you have them on completion of the transaction. In the meantime we can start proceedings if this is OK with you Mr Adams?" Catherine reached across the large desk and handed Daniel her passport and identification papers.

She rose slowly from her chair and leaned forward to reach the silver frame on Daniels desk. She gently turned the picture slightly towards Daniel. "Mr Adams, could you tell me who the young lady is in the photograph?" Daniel took the picture frame in his hands. Staring intently at the photograph for a few seconds, he tenderly replaced it in its original home. "The young lady in the picture was my girlfriend Rachael Bryce. She died tragically in a hit and run accident over 23 years ago. She was with her best friend Susie

Kruger. They were both killed in the accident. The culprits were never apprehended, but I always had my suspicions. Nothing was ever proven although there was, in my mind, enough evidence for a conviction. It happened the night both girls walked home from an evening out; they were mowed down, on the pavement and left to die. Eventually they were taken to hospital, where Rachael died in the ambulance and Susie a little later. It was a terrible time for everyone in Rachael's life. Her parents have never recovered and her friends, and myself included, feel exactly the same. We just learnt to live with it. If only the girls would have accepted my offer of a lift home that night. It could have been very different."

"Well. I mustn't dwell on the past, but there isn't a day goes by that I don't think of her, and of course Susie her best friend.

"It was common knowledge then that Mr and Mrs Kruger took care of you Catherine whilst Susie went back to university. Rachael always said what a beautiful baby you were. Ironically about the same time the terrible accident occurred whilst Mr and Mrs Kruger were on holiday in the Cayman Islands. I understand now that there was an explosion on their hired boat. Possibly a gas explosion, but again this was never proven. Their bodies were never recovered. Miraculously you were not on the boat at the time. This of course, saved your life. But it was thought that you were on the boat, and lost along with your grandparents."

"I am sure your Aunt Izzy has spoken of this many times and you are completely aware of all the facts. The necklace she is wearing is one of a pair. The other one belonged to Susie. The necklace will come to you one day, if it is not already in your possession."

As Catherine focused on the picture of Rachael directly in front of her, her mind wandered… and once more she found herself in front of a very large Colonial house. The same house she had seen many times before. "What is this place? I've got to know, it's obviously the key to unlocking this mystery, if I could just make out the writing on the board…" It was summer it felt warm and somehow safe. She could almost smell the sweet scents of the stocks surrounding the entrance to this grand house. Catherine found herself walking towards the open large front door. She still couldn't make out the writing on the board but she could hear her name being called again, very faintly. As she walked closer it echoed of a past memory. What was this memory? Where was she? There standing directly in front of her was a figure of a young woman. Was this Rachael, beckoning her to come closer, pointing to the wooden twisting staircase of this large rambling house; was she to follow her?

"Are you alright Catherine?" Daniel asked, looking quite concerned. "You seemed to have drifted somewhere for a moment. I hope I'm not upsetting you in any way?"

Catherine gradually focused on what Daniel was saying, and replied, "No, really I'm fine, just a bit dizzy; I'll be Ok in a moment, thank you." Daniel answered the phone on his desk and walked over to the window.

Izzy looked at Catherine, knowing full well what had happened. "We are getting closer to the truth Izzy. I've got to find this grand Colonial house. I know it's significant. When we are finished here I'm going straight to the library to see if I can find anything that may help. There has got to be something there, something that we have overlooked..."

Chapter 44
2010

Brody picked up his 'secure line' phone and dialled the number he had hidden away. He'd been saving the number for just this moment; if and when it did eventually arrive. After only a short wait, the call was answered; "what is your security code please."

Brody had the code ready, and now he was completely sure this was the right thing to do. "32-46-5384," he replied.

"That's correct Mr Myers, please proceed, I shall put you through to your contact."

The line clicked and went quiet for what seemed like an age. "Hello Brody, you've made the right decision, we can at last put this guy away for good. I need you to confirm that you will be at the rendezvous at the exact time, place and date that we had previously arranged. There cannot be any mistakes. We don't want Todd Clayton to get wind of anything unusual or out of the ordinary. Do I make myself clear Brody – no mistakes?"

"Yes perfectly – I won't let you down. But how will I recognise you?"

"I'll be the guy with an earpiece, a black and yellow striped tie, and of course – a gun!"

Brody carefully replaced the telephone receiver. "Too late to turn back now, but hell, I don't want to, he deserves all he is about to get."

"Tomorrow then, 1.30 pm at the rendezvous," Brody confirmed to himself.

Chapter 45
2010

Daniel was happy in the thought that everything was progressing according to plan. The monies were now secure in the two new accounts. It was quite a shock when he informed Catherine that someone had been extremely savvy investing part of the account, splitting it and transferring monies periodically into another account. These accounts sat there and had gradually amassed over the years. Her total wealth now was a staggering $30,520,670!! She had walked into the bank with a bank balance in Britain of approximately £524.00 and would potentially be walking out a millionaire!

"He is going to pursue me, I know it. Todd will do anything to get his hands on this money Izzy."

"It's not going to be easy Catherine, I never said it would be but he's not going to get away with anything anymore," Aunt Izzy said quite determined; "you know that I have friends with a great deal of influence dear. There is something looming; he will be out of harm's way soon, as long as all goes well without a hitch."

Catherine knew what Izzy meant, she was now comfortable with the knowledge that her aunt was an agent or spy, or whatever she liked to call herself, but she wasn't comfortable with the now all too obvious outcome that was likely to follow.

"Well, Catherine, thank you for your continued confidence in myself and the Credit Suisse Bank of Boston. If there is anything that I can be of assistance with, please let me know I will be only too happy to help. You are now a very rich woman. Do you have any plans to what you will do with the money, investments of some sort, bonds maybe, or building a property portfolio? That could be a very lucrative option" Daniel informed Catherine.

"No, I hadn't thought that far ahead, but this money is 'blood money'. I will have to give it a great deal of thought."

"I understand," Daniel replied. "Here is my personal card. Ring me anytime, day or night, if there is anything bothering you, I am a good listener, there may also be other matters you wish to discuss?"

"Mr Adams, it couldn't have been an easy task for you, getting all the documents and information needed to finalise these accounts. I'm sure there were moments of trepidation for you, of which I am extremely grateful for your insistence in continuing your enquiries regarding these accounts. I have waited a long time for this moment and it's finally here. Really, my sincere thanks to you and your colleagues," Catherine said emotionally.

She glanced down at the bank statement. Her hand was trembling. It read like a winning lottery ticket! It was inconceivable that she was now the recipient of this extremely large amount of money, far larger than anyone could ever want or need. She had plenty of time to decide the best course of action that she would take – plenty of time! But one thing was for sure, a tidy sum would be given to charity, the least she could do, for her family who made this possible for her future, namely her birth mother and grandparents. Of course she would make sure Aunt Izzy was well looked after.

Catherine shook Daniel Adams' hand. "I will see you the day after tomorrow Mr Adams at 10 am when we can discuss my investment options. Goodbye and thank you again."

As Catherine rose from her seat, she glanced once again at the photograph of the young girl on Daniel Adams desk. "What is Rachael trying to tell me?" A movement behind her brought her thoughts sharply back to the present... "Catherine we should have lunch now, and we can talk further. I want to discuss with you what's going to happen in the next few days," Izzy confirmed.

Catherine was not scared easily, but even she had to admit to herself, she was worried what the eventual outcome of all this might be.

"OK Izzy, let's do lunch, my treat," Catherine replied. "Tomorrow I'm going to the library to search back 23 years to the moment of the hit and run accident and try to find out what really happened at that time. Rachael is trying to tell me something. I must find out the truth before it's too late. Maybe a visit to Rachael's parents may help?"

"Mmm.. You would have to be very discreet and careful how you approached the subject, you wouldn't want to upset them anymore than necessary dear. They have endured such a lot over the years," Izzy replied.

"I know," Catherine agreed; "for sure."

Catherine and Izzy left the Bank and made their way downtown. They found the perfect Bistro for lunch and Aunt Izzy began to relay to Catherine the events that were shortly to take place, if all went well and according to plane ...

Chapter 46
2010

The next morning Catherine woke with the lark. A busy day lay ahead if she was to achieve everything she had set her mind on to do. The aroma of the freshly brewed coffee drifted fragrantly up the stairs and she could almost taste her Aunt Izzy's blueberry pancakes she was busy preparing downstairs in the kitchen.

Hurriedly Catherine showered and dressed in blue jeans and a casual pale blue knit sweater. As she drew back the heavy white lace curtains, the early morning sunlight flooded into the bedroom, and she was pleasantly surprised to see that it was a beautiful day. The sea mist rose in the far distance, creating a blue hue across the peaceful countryside; it was a perfect day for a stroll to the local library.

"Catherine, breakfast is ready," Aunt Izzy shouted softly from the bottom of the stairs. "Ok, be down in a sec," Catherine replied placing a notebook and pen in her bag for jotting down information she may come across at the library. "I hope I find something today, and it's not a complete waste of time. It's got to be there, something that was overlooked way back all those years ago. I'm going to find it if it takes all day," Catherine thought to herself.

She knew Izzy would want to visit the library with her. She didn't mind. She had got used to her being around, and relying on her, probably more than she ever intended to. Izzy was a whole new entity since Catherine discovered her hidden past. She wasn't sure how far and deep the knowledge or influence Izzy had went within the CIA but she knew that she had come to depend on her more and more for everything that related to her dark past and hopefully bright future.

Catherine sneaked a quick glance towards Izzy. "You know, she may look quirky but boy was she quick in mind if not in body," Catherine muttered to herself. She often overlooked the fact that she was, after all, in her 80s, but no one would ever have guessed it.

Both Catherine and Izzy walked at a slow pace towards the library. The day was sultry, with a clear blue cloudless sky. The only breeze that could be felt was soft and blew gently through the branches of the ash and sycamore trees that lined the road leading to the library.

"What a beautiful day dear," Izzy announced, taking her large floppy straw hat from her head as they entered the library.

"Yes it's a pity to be spending time indoors on a gorgeous day like today, but this is far more important a task for us to look into than sitting in the park!" Izzy could see that Catherine was anxious but determined to see this through to the end, and nothing was going to stop her.

Catherine walked towards the reception desk in the main lobby of the library. A middle-aged woman with short brown hair and steel-rimmed spectacles spoke to Catherine. "Can I help you?" "Yes, could you please tell me where we will find past records and events which took place about 20 years ago?" The receptionist looked away. She took several books handed to her from a pretty young girl, no more than five years of age. She stamped the books and handed them back to her. "Thank you" the small child gestured and left smiling, holding her mother's hand. "I am sorry, just one moment please and I'll be with you," the middle-aged woman replied. "We've got in the wrong queue as usual Izzy," Catherine remarked, smiling annoyingly as the librarian looked down over her steel-rimmed glasses directly at Catherine. "Well you will find everything you need on the first floor; old newspaper articles, events, births, deaths, etc," she said. "I do hope you find what you are looking for."

"Thank you," Catherine replied.

Izzy and Catherine turned and walked away along the dark red patterned, rather worn carpet towards the stairs that led to the first floor of the library. They climbed the stairs, and made their way along a dark narrow corridor. On the walls hung old photographs of the library of days long gone, barely recognisable now, but nonetheless, fascinating and they held Catherine and Izzy's attention for several moments. Finally they arrived at the double doors marked 'Archives'. "Here we are Catherine." Izzy pushed the doors open to reveal an area full of large square wooden tables scattered around the room with computers and keyboards resting on them, spaced out evenly to accommodate at least six people on each table.

There were shelves upon shelves of books, and files and journals. "Gosh where do we start?" Catherine said.

Izzy looked around the familiar surroundings. She knew exactly where to go and where to look. "Over here dear, this computer will bring up virtually everything from that era." Catherine sat next to Izzy, and they started scrolling back in time to the 70s' and 80s' and newspaper articles connected to Yale University.

"So much information, we'll never get through all of this in one day Izzy," Catherine declared, despair creeping into her voice.

"Yes we will, have a little patience and a little faith dear," Izzy replied, who clearly had the better share.

Several hours passed. Two cappuccinos, tuna and mayo sandwiches, and fruit juices later, Catherine literally shouted – "It's here I think," as she flicked backwards and forwards through the newspaper clippings of the day. "Yes, here it is Izzy. Look, the heading reads: Two young women students at Yale University; killed in a hit and run accident on wet road conditions… girls rushed to hospital, one DOA and the other died shortly after. It goes on to say, only one set of parents were in attendance at the funeral due to the untimely death of Susie Kruger's parents only weeks before the hit and run, leaving only a brother and sister of Susie Kruger, to mourn their loss.

"Where are my Aunt and Uncle now?"Catherine asked. Izzy remained very quiet, not commenting flicking forward, studying painstakingly slowly, future articles before clicking onto the death certificates for both girls issued at the time.

"Here this is what I was looking for Catherine," Izzy commented. They both sat quite motionless as they began to study the death certificate, firstly for Rachael. The certificate shown on the computer screen was very faint, and only just legible. Tears began to well up uncontrollably in Catherine's eyes. It was all she could do to refrain from losing her composure, looking at the Death Certificate of a girl that she had felt she had come to know so well, yet had died tragically along with Susie, Catherine's own birth mother; next, the death certificate for Susie Kruger. It was barely legible. They could just make out the date of birth, mother, father, place of birth, but date of death... however hard both Catherine and Izzy tried, they couldn't make it out.

"We'll print off these articles, clippings and certificates, we've found, but we will have to go to the office for Registrar of Births and Deaths to get a copy of Susie's death certificate, if that is what you want Catherine?" Aunt Izzy asked.

"Yes it is Izzy, perhaps we'll go tomorrow."

Izzy held Catherine's hand. She could see she was upset; "look dear, there is a very good friend of mine who works at the Yale University Library on Elm Street known as the "Laz." It's a popular 24hr. study space. I know he will be only too pleased to look into this for us further. He can, if anyone can get hold of this information. So before we go rushing off anywhere, leave it with me and I will ring him when we get home." "Ok Izzy," Catherine replied, hoping all the information they had gathered was enough to go on for now.

Izzy felt awful. She had held back a secret from Catherine for so long now, but to ensure the outcome was favourable for Catherine, she had no choice. This was the only way forward.

Something was still niggling at the back of Catherine's mind. What was it, what was she missing?

Chapter 47
2010

Brody let the phone ring continuously until it eventually stopped. He knew it was Todd. He knew exactly how the conversation would go. Questioning and badgering him into submission until he couldn't stand it any longer, and would go along with anything and everything Todd ordered. But it was different this time. He would not question anything that was asked of him. Brody knew what the outcome would be. He was grateful to at last be rid of Todd's clutches, even if it meant he may have to answer for it.

The phone rang again. Brody answered the call – "Hi Todd. All set for tomorrow?" Brody asked.

"Yes, at last I'm going to get the money owed to me. That bitch had better give me the codes and account number, or it could get very messy Brody. Daughter or no daughter, she owes me."

"Ok Todd, but you promised no heavy stuff," Brody replied authentically. "Well I've changed my mind. I need that money now, and she is not going to stop me getting my hands on it."

Brody knew once Todd was in that sort of mood, nothing would get in his way. He was so like his father, no grey area, only black or white! What a family. How did he ever get involved with this maniac? To think he could be running for Office sent shivers down Brody's spine.

Brody continued to appease Todd, but not to the extent he would get suspicious. "Everything is in place for tomorrow," Brody replied. "Are all the backup guys ready," Todd asked impatiently. "Yes, they will all be at the rendezvous at the given time," Brody reluctantly agreed.

"Good. I'll see you tomorrow then. For fuck sake, don't be late," Todd yelled down the phone. "Everything depends on tomorrow so don't fuck up."

Todd hung up without a goodbye. Brody was used to that. "Ignorant bastard," Brody thought to himself. "Your day is about to come. Let's hope it all goes well, and he doesn't get wind of the plot," Brody muttered to himself. "I can't wait to see his face. Please God let it happen without a hitch."

Brody knew the great risk he was taking. He had somebody he knew he could trust on the outside, coming in. Someone he had known for many years, and had kept in touch with and was now about to surface...

Chapter 48
2010

The newly painted old picket fence, still grey and white, shone brightly as the late afternoon sun hugged its wooden panels. Catherine sat next to Izzy on the porch swing that overlooked the lake. "I remember this wonderful view across the lake on so many of my holidays with you when I was a child," Catherine said. "Nobody can take that away from me."

"Yes, it was a special time for both of us, getting to know each other, memories I will hold forever in my heart Catherine," Izzy replied. "Let's hope we have many more."

"I'm sure we will Izzy," Catherine replied as they swung gently on the porch swing looking over the peaceful lake, the sun gradually disappearing beyond the trees.

"I've telephoned my colleague Jonathan Macey at the Berkeley College, and he has kindly agreed to delve further into the death certificate for your mother," Izzy stated. "I hope this is not going to be too upsetting for you, as we dig further into the past, you never know what we may find. "Nothing is ever what it seems dear.""

The chill in the air prompted Izzy and Catherine to go indoors. Catherine couldn't help wondering what Izzy had meant by "Nothing is ever what it seems." She pushed the thought to the back of her mind and Aunt Izzy agreed to make them hot chocolate, with her homemade ginger cookies. Catherine was thankful for the distraction. A lot had happened, maybe too much to digest in one day, as she snuggled up on the sofa with Izzy's patchwork crochet blanket, drifting into a light sleep... Again Catherine found herself back at the old Colonial House. But this time she was standing at the top of the winding staircase.

Directly in front of her was Rachael, beckoning her to follow. Catherine could distinctly see the necklace around Rachael's neck; "it almost seemed to sparkle, Catherine thought mesmerised as the beams of coloured prisms could be seen all around Rachael now, as she led the way forward. She looked so beautiful and serene; Catherine followed. Slowly, gently she watched as Rachael glided through the dimly lit corridor. The pungent perfume of the freshly cut coloured hocks in a vase that stood on a white wooden consul table, was strong as they passed slowly along the passageway until Rachael suddenly stopped.

Rachael smiled within as it lit up her face. She had stopped outside a large door towards the end of the corridor that was slightly ajar. She pointed to the door. Catherine was straining to see the plaque on the door, as she moved closer and closer...

"Catherine, wake up dear, hot chocolate and cookies, just what we need after a day like today, eh?"

Catherine slowly opened her eyes. "I was having such a lovely dream Izzy, Rachael was there again, in the old Colonial House, trying to show me something, a room I think. The room was at the end of a long corridor, but I couldn't see the plaque on the door. I'm getting closer Izzy, I know it; I feel it. The dreams don't frighten me anymore. They are getting less frequent now but much more vivid and I think I am about to learn the truth one way or another. Just a few more dreams... let's hope it works that way."

Izzy knew it was only a matter of time before Catherine was fully aware of the truth. She would have many questions for Izzy and she must have the answers ready for her, like it or not.

Although there were many questions Izzy could answer, the house was not one of them. Izzy knew nothing of the Old Colonial House, and was just as bewildered and puzzled about the connection as Catherine was. She was determined to find the truth about the house for Catherine's sake.

Izzy handed Catherine a large mug of hot chocolate, and several ginger cookies. "It seems you could now be onto something dear," Izzy replied.

"We just need to find this old 'Colonial House.' I think the house is the key to the truth, and the sooner we find it the better," Catherine yawned.

"It looked like a rest home maybe, I'm not entirely sure, but that's a good place to start. We could look on the internet. I might recognise it, you never know," Catherine said.

"It's a long shot, but worth a try dear," Izzy replied.

"Let's do it tomorrow dear, and get an early night, as you know we have a meeting with Daniel Adams at 10 tomorrow to finalise everything."

"Ok, it can wait 'till tomorrow, its waited all this time, another day will make little or no difference," Catherine replied, sipping her mug of hot chocolate...

Chapter 49
2010

Daniel Adams glanced at his watch. The time was 10.20 am. "I wonder what's keeping Miss Morgan. Her appointment was at 10 am?"

Daniel thought himself a pretty good judge of character; he felt it was somewhat uncharacteristic of her to be this late. Picking up the intercom phone on his desk he pressed the green button to connect to his secretary. "Can you please call Miss Morgan on her cell, to make sure she hasn't forgotten her appointment?" Daniel requested. "Yes, of course Mr Adams, straight away." After a short while the phone on Daniel's desk rang. "I haven't been able to reach Miss Morgan at home or on her cell sir," his secretary stated. "OK, thank you." Daniel replaced the receiver. The time was now 10.35.

Daniel dialled John Colbert on his secure line. "Hi Daniel, how's it going, well I hope?" he replied.

"Yep, but might have a slight problem. Look John, have you heard anything, anything at all that may jeopardise the safety of the accounts being finalised for Miss Morgan? She had an appointment this morning to sign the remaining paperwork, at 10 o'clock but hasn't shown. She isn't answering her cell either."

"I haven't heard anything definite, but word has it that something big is about to manifest itself. Both forces want to corner Todd Clayton now. I don't believe they are gonna mess about any longer. Have a word with Izabelle, she may know something. She knows more than she lets on! In the meantime I'll get in touch with my source and get back to you ASAP!" John Colbert confirmed.

"Ok mate, thanks for the insight," Daniel replied.

***

It was 9.30 am the morning of the final meeting with Daniel Adams to finalise the account that Catherine was about to inherit. Parking their car in the underground car park, Catherine and Izzy walked slowly, chatting as they went, towards the glass revolving doors of the bank. Suddenly from out of nowhere, two men approached them from behind; one grabbed Catherine and the other Aunt Izzy; as much as they struggled to get free, they couldn't. The men were too big and too strong for them. "How could this be happening to us in broad daylight? This isn't real. This only happens in the movies!!" Catherine thought to herself. Panic replaced any rational thinking...

"Let go of me," Catherine shouted at the top of her voice. "What do you want?"

"You," was the reply from a big, burly unshaven middle-aged man. "There is someone who has waited a long time to finally meet you, and of course your Aunt Izabelle as well," blurted the unsavoury individual holding Catherine tightly by both arms, rendering her unable to move.

"Catherine don't fight him, it would be futile, and dangerous," whispered Izzy, being held by an equally large, heavy weight individual. "Wherever they are taking us, it's the end game, I think you are about to finally meet your father Catherine."

Izzy could see the shock of her last sentence, sinking in and etching on Catherine's face. "I don't want to meet him," gasped Catherine. "I don't want anything to do with him, he's a cruel, evil bastard and as far as I am concerned, I don't have a father."

"Get in the car, and stop yapping, you'll be there soon enough," shouted the smaller of the two burly individuals. Both Izzy and Catherine's hands were bound behind them, tied securely. "No chance of getting out of this easily," Catherine thought, trying hard to release her hands, but to no avail.

They were tumbled into a black 4 x 4 Range Rover. Windows blacked out, and a glass screen sectioned off the front seats from the rear. The two kidnappers got in the front of the vehicle. "We don't want to hear a peep from either of you before we reach our destination, do you understand?" They closed the front screen and locked all the doors.

"Great Izzy," Catherine sighed. "What now? How are we going to get out of this one?"

Izzy took a deep breath, and tried to calm Catherine. "Trust me Catherine, it is not as bad as it might seem. There are forces out there working against Todd Clayton, have been for years, under cover and out of sight and off the grid.

"I don't know where they are taking us, but you can be sure my contact does, and hopefully he will be there with Todd Clayton. He is going to get the biggest shock of his useless life. Of course all he wants are the codes and account numbers, which he thinks we are going to give him. I have dummy codes and account numbers ready for him and his associates. By the time he realises they are completely useless, it should be 'game over.'

"God I hope you're right Izzy, for both our sakes," Catherine whispered.

Time passed slowly as they travelled from the freeway into the suburbs. They drove for several miles down countless slip roads and narrow alley ways passing dumpsters and graffiti-scribbled buildings. They turned eventually into a narrow alleyway, run down, tumbleweeds blowing in the breeze and lined with old rusty cars and car body parts.

Catherine looked at Izzy. "I know this alleyway, I've been here before; I mean I've seen this before... Look the old broken lamp above the entrance to the garage... and over there... Andy's Autos – the sign, broken and half hanging off... This is where the car was taken that was involved in the hit and run accident all those years ago. This is where it was repaired!!!"

Chapter 50
2010

The black 4 x 4 carrying Catherine and Izzy eventually slowed down as it came to an abrupt halt. The two men in the front of the car sat in silence for what seemed an age. A cell phone rang several times before it was answered. It had one of those ringtones, so embarrassing, Catherine thought. "I don't know why anyone would want 'Icona Pop' singing 'I Don't Care, I Love It' blaring out of their mobile phone, every time they received a call"; but then Catherine had always considered herself a bit old-fashioned and out of the loop!

"Right OK boss, will do, don't worry, we've got 'em here," was the response to the call. Both men got out of the 4 x 4 and made their way to the back of the vehicle.

"Get out of the car and don't make a sound, do you get it?" spat the large guy. Catherine and Izzy were manhandled out of the black 4 x 4 and led up to the lock-up garage. The badly fitted wooden weathered door slid noisily across its hinges. It was dark and dreary, dusty and damp inside the lock-up, and a musty aroma hung in the air. A hazy beam of light made its way through the small broken window up high, on the far side of the garage, giving a gloomy and eerie feeling to the now relic shell of a lock up, that once was probably a hive of activity. There it was in the corner, the old brown worn leather armchair and directly above it, still hanging on the badly plastered wall, was the old clock. The time had not changed. It still read 1.35!! "So it wasn't working then and it's still not working now," Catherine murmured under her breath.

Izzy could see the recognition on Catherine's face. Looking at each other they knew whatever was about to happen in the next few minutes was not going to be good. A strange calm came over Catherine in the knowledge that there was nothing she or Izzy could do to change what was about to take place.

"Sit down," shouted the unshaven guy, pushing Catherine and Izzy onto two separate white plastic fold-up chairs. There were now seven men in place, just standing around waiting. Most wore dark suits, white shirts and ties, with strategically placed earpieces. Some wore manual clothes, but all were on the payroll of Todd Clayton, that Catherine was certain of.

There was one member of Todd Clayton's staff who had stood alone with his back to Catherine and Izzy for best part of the time. He turned and walked directly over to where she was sitting. Catherine tried her hardest not to look surprised. She peered at Izzy who was looking away, making sure there was no immediate eye contact between them, for fear of giving the game away.

"Are you sure these are tied securely?" he shouted to the other members of staff, as he knelt down in the pretence of examining the cords that held Catherine's hands tied securely behind her back. "Don't say a word, and do not recognise me Catherine," he whispered, "your life may depend on it."

"This is unbelievable," Catherine thought. "What is he doing here? Why is he involved with these people?" Izzy looked directly at Martin Castona without a shadow of recognition, as he tested her tied hands, just to be sure. Izzy had known Martin for many years, and over the years things had become more complicated. It wasn't possible for her, in her position, to let Catherine know the real truth. It was too dangerous. She had no choice but to deceive her. Izzy knew she would have a lot of explaining to do, come the day!

A car could be heard pulling up outside the lock-up. The engine ceased, two doors were heard slamming shut, and an immobiliser initiated. Several sets of footsteps could be heard approaching the garage. They stopped directly outside. A short conversation took place between two men before the footsteps could be heard approaching, walking slowly into the lock-up. Catherine and Izzy sat with their backs to the newcomers. Finally the two men walked forward towards the old wooden bench in the centre of the garage.

Each man was roughly 45 years of age. They stood side by side at the bench, about ten feet away from Catherine and Izzy. The taller of the two was smart, with dark blonde hair. He wore a dark grey sports jacket, white open neck shirt, and black leather gloves. "He is good looking in a school boy way," Catherine thought, "but his eyes are cold and steely. Is this my father? Is this the man I have waited all my life to see?" Catherine looked directly at him, whilst he placed his briefcase and papers on the wooden bench. The other man wore a dark suit, white shirt and tie, the same as the other members of staff. He was about the same age; his hair darker in colour. He didn't stand as tall as the first newcomer, but he had a much larger physique, and a softer kinder face.

The taller of the two men took off his black leather gloves and placed them on the bench. He took out paper documents from his briefcase and rested them on the surface.

Turning around very slowly and deliberately to face Catherine and Izzy, he introduced himself. "I am Todd Clayton, as you both may well be aware by now, and you have been brought here because you have something that belongs to me," he stated.

"There will be no negotiations, you will give me the account numbers and codes, or face the consequences …. And yes I am your father Catherine Morgan, but don't think that will make the slightest bit of difference to the outcome. You and your aunt will be perfectly safe as long as you do as I say. Do I make myself clear? You mean nothing to me. You are a means to an end. I paid off your mother and her parents, all those years ago, to have an abortion but she deceived me and went ahead with the birth.

"So now it's payback time Catherine, what do you say to that…?"

Chapter 51
2010

Catherine looked across to where Izzy was seated. She was seething inside with anger. Now was the time to tell Todd Clayton exactly what she thought of him. She had waited a long time for this moment but feared for her and Izzy's life and was very wary of him. He seemed remarkably unstable. She didn't want to antagonise him in any way, in case it provoked an unavoidable response, and a situation she and Izzy couldn't get out of. Nothing anybody could advise at this point would make the slightest bit of difference, it was up to her now; it was her say.

"If you think for one minute that I, or my aunt, are going to give you those codes and account numbers you are very much mistaken," Catherine shouted at Todd. "You've got as much chance of acquiring that information from us as you giving me the definition of black matter in the universe!!!" A wry smile breached Martin Castona's face.

Todd stood silent. His face turned red with anger. "You think you're clever don't you Catherine, but you will never win over me! Ask anyone here. They will tell you, I always get what I want, and I want those codes!!!"

Catherine and Izzy glanced at each other, both thinking the same thing. What was that muffled kafuffle outside the large garage doors leading to the alleyway? Could Todd Clayton not hear it? Was he deaf? But before Todd had the chance to warn anyone, they were in, everywhere; an army of armed men, the police and The FBI.

Catherine could see that Martin Castona was now running the show. He was in charge. He winked at Brody – the signal to grab Todd Clayton. They wrestled him to the ground, held him down until the uniformed police took over. There were at least 20 armed police surrounding the seven men in Todd Claytons employ. The FBI agents followed, ten of them in black uniforms, worn over their bulletproof vests, displaying the undeniable FBI logo displayed prominently on their backs. They ran quickly forward, brandishing firearms and shouting, "On the floor now!" Several shots of warning rang out. "Everyone get down on the floor NOW!!!"

"Ok Todd it's over for you pal. Tell your men to put down their guns. You're completely surrounded. Don't do anything foolish, it will only go against you at your trial. I've waited a long, long time for this moment you bastard. I've had to endure your arrogance and cold bloodedness all these years working for you, but it's finally over, the end of the road for you bud!!!" Brody said defiantly.

"Well done Brody. You've done the right thing" Martin shouted.

"Yes it's been a long time coming" Brody replied. "We've all had to wait many years for this day, and you're going down for a long stretch Todd, you can bet on that."

The two police officers got Todd Clayton to his feet. Although shocked and dishevelled, he slowly and unnervingly replied. "You'll never get away with this Brody, and as for you, talking directly to Martin Castona, you may have only been in my employ for a short time, and you may have fooled me this time, but be assured, you won't get away with this. You'll have to have eyes in the back of your head from now on," Todd replied slowly and deliberately. "I'll fucking get you for this, you mark my words if I don't!"

The FBI rounded up all the members of staff in Todd Clayton's employment. Their hands now bound with the all too familiar plastic ties. Looking angry and confused, his members of staff were forcibly bundled into the alleyway by the FBI Agents. One by one they were then placed into the FBI vehicles and police vans and driven off at speed, down the alleyway – the vehicles' sirens blazing as they were seen disappearing into the afternoon sunshine.

That just left Todd Clayton. The two police officers held him tightly for fear of him escaping. They escorted Todd outside into the alley way as he wriggled to get free. He took one look at the Black Maria sitting on the tarmac with its barred windows, waiting silently in the alleyway and he murmured to himself. "This is not going to be my life now or for the foreseeable future if I have anything to do with it." He stepped up into the waiting Black Maria. The door was slammed and locked behind him. The two police officers banged on the side of the vehicle, signalling all ok to go. Todd Clayton could be seen, hands clasped in desperation on the bars of the window of the Black Maria as it sped away.

"You knew this was about to happen didn't you Izzy?" Catherine said. "Why didn't you tell me?"

"I couldn't dear. It might have jeopardised the whole operation we have been working on for the last five years. The plan had been set in motion many years ago. We all knew about Todd Clayton's intentions, the FBI, the CIA, the present government, and many more people who had fallen on hard times because of him. But his father is still a very powerful man, and has many friends in high places; this was the only way to trap him. I'm so sorry Catherine. We have a lot to talk about dear, many things that you are completely unaware of. I know I've said this before, but it is time you knew the truth, nothing barred, but again best left 'till tomorrow, when we both have had some rest, and I will tell you everything, everything I know about your family, past and present."

Martin and Brody made their way over to where Catherine and Izzy were patiently waiting to be released from the ties wound around their wrists.

"Hello Catherine," Martin Castonna winked. "Look I know I owe you an explanation and I'm really sorry to surprise and frighten you with this rowdy ruckus that ensued here, but there was no other way. The operation was planned for today. There is a lot I have to explain to you, and when this is all over I will tell you everything. I promise. We'll have a glass of Chardonnay, and no doubt you will have lots of questions for me." Martin gently untied both Izzy and Catherine's hands. "I'll call you later Catherine, and schedule a day to visit; if that's ok?"

"I'm going to leave you now with these two FBI agents Catherine. They will see you safely home and will also stay posted outside your house this evening, to help you feel a little safer. Please don't worry about what Todd Clayton threatened, he has no power now. Even his father cannot help him. We have too many witnesses in the witness protection programme to testify against him in a court of law, and I personally cannot wait to see him behind bars for a very long time."

Catherine stood up from the white plastic garden chair she had sat on for the past half an hour and looked around the lock-up garage. "This could have all been so different," she thought. "Izzy, thank you for keeping me safe, without you and Martin there may have been a completely different outcome. I really can't believe that I have waited all this time to meet Todd Clayton, my father; what a disappointment to find out he is such an evil man." If I had a gun now I think I would shoot him myself! Catherine said. She was angry and disillusioned and felt greatly let down by him.

Izzy smiled. She knew she and Martin Castona had a lot of explaining to do the next day or so. "Let's go home dear, we have a lot to talk about tomorrow don't we...?"

Chapter 52
2010

John Colbert travelled swiftly, passing through the glass revolving doors into the Credit Swiss Bank, narrowly missing a young woman as he walked into the foyer of the bank. Urgently he pressed the button outside the glass elevator. He stepped quickly inside, hurriedly closing the doors. The elevator sped up to the fifth floor which seemed to take forever to reach its destination. He stepped outside and into the hallway, hastily making his way to where Daniel Adams' office was located.

Winking at his secretary, he ran past her desk and straight into Daniel's office without knocking. "John, what the hell is wrong. You look shocked - what's happened?" John Colbert, pulled up a leather chair, sank slowly down, caught his breath and proceeded to tell Daniel the information as it was unfolded to him moments ago; the demise of Todd Clayton.

"Are you sure? Is this on the level? I can't believe it, Todd Clayton in jail?" Daniel Adams sat back in his chair and reflected back to his Yale University days when life was much simpler and Todd Clayton had the world at his feet. Rich parents, a bright future; a future Daniel and few of his friends thought they would ever experience. Where did it all go wrong?

"I can't say I feel sorry for him, he'll get what he deserves, and not before time by all accounts, eh John?"

"Yeah you're right bud, not before time," was the sarcastic reply. "Well Danny, what happens now?"

Daniel Adams thought for a moment before answering the loaded question. "This could be complicated. If Todd Clayton was to inform the authorities of this account, proving the money was given from Government funds, and not a personal account, all those years ago, under false pretences and without the knowledge of the proper authorities, including the IRS, this could be bad for Catherine Morgan. He could do this just to spite her, knowing he would never be getting his hands on the money as he intended. She would have to prove she is his daughter, and if she was to deny this fact, she would only be entitled to a percentage of the original account; a 'finders' fee would in all probability, apply. The paper trail would then end there.

"Would Catherine be entitled to this money that had gained compound interest over the years in the account that was invested by the Krugers years ago? As long as it remained unknown and hidden, who knows?" Daniel pondered.

"I personally think he might try and strike up a deal with the authorities to lessen his sentence. It just depends of the origin of the money. Of course this would mean him giving them information on the account in Catherine's name, and if it was confirmed that the original $2,000,000 came from Government funds and not personal money, this would not be healthy for him or his father," Daniel replied. "Also if it WAS found to be 'Government funds' it would immediately incriminate his father, and that would be something Todd would want to avoid at all costs, knowing the history between the pair of them."

"On the other hand, if he thought Catherine would inherit the money he could come after her for it, if he was to be released early for good behaviour, and of course depending on which Brief he used. Mark my words, the Brief he employed would be the best dirty money could buy!!"

"Yeah, food for thought Daniel, we'll just have to wait and see what pans out eh?" John Colbert sighed. He stretched out his hand to shake Daniel's hand in friendship; "a job, well done bud."

"Yes thanks, pal" Daniel replied. "If you here of anything else that may help, please get in touch." "Be sure of it Danny," catch you later. Daniel Adams immediately instructed his secretary to contact Catherine Morgan to arrange a meeting to discuss the best way forward, just as soon as it was humanly possible!

Chapter 53
2010

The distant sound of a phone ringing broke the silence between Izzy and Catherine. They arrived home safely and were sitting quietly in the lounge, drinking whisky to calm their nerves, not a word uttered between them.

"I'll go," Catherine said, getting up from the sofa and making her way to the kitchen. "Hello," she replied, balancing the phone receiver on her shoulder whilst finishing her whisky.

"Hello Catherine," its Daniel. "I'm sorry to ring you at home at a time like this. I've just heard what happened earlier today. It must have been a great shock for you and your aunt. I am so sorry. You must feel very nervous and exhausted at the moment, so I will try to keep it brief. There are matters that we need to talk over, and decisions you have to make. Therefore, the sooner the better, so I was wondering if I could call on you tomorrow morning to finalise these issues? Say about 11 am?"

"Yes I don't see why not," Catherine replied. "You are right there are important decisions I have to make tomorrow. The sooner we get this over the better. I'm not sure I want this money; it's blood money. There have been too many deaths surrounding its existence; I don't think I want any part of it."

Daniel hesitated before answering. "Look Catherine, I know it's none of my business, but your mother and grandparents died, and in all probability, were killed trying to give you a better future. I'm not sure giving up on the money involved at this stage would be the right way forward. Wait 'till tomorrow, sleep on it and we can discuss this in detail. I have an idea that may be of interest to you."

"Ok Daniel, I'll see you tomorrow at 11 am, here at Aunt Izzy's," Catherine replied. "Do you know the address?"

"Yes Catherine, I do. I have visited your aunt on several occasions in the past. I'll see you tomorrow at 11 am. Goodbye for now Catherine."

Catherine replaced the receiver. "Mmm – how come he has been here visiting Izzy before? Maybe it's got something to do with her days as a spy in the CIA, she thought?" laughing to herself, slightly baffled as she walked back into the lounge, where Aunt Izzy was finishing her whisky.

"That was Daniel Adams on the phone. He's coming here at 11 tomorrow morning to discuss the account and how best to proceed," Catherine spoke hesitantly. She didn't know whether to mention the fact that Daniel had spoken of visiting her at home here on several occasions in the past. She didn't mention it. Best left alone for the time being she thought. There was too much going on in her life. Another revelation could easily tip her over the edge.

"That's good dear," Izzy replied. "There will be enough time tomorrow morning before Daniel gets here to let you into all the secrets about your family's dark past, as I promised I would and how it is likely to change your life completely..."

Chapter 54
2010

It was 6.30 am the following morning. Catherine's sleep had been restless most of the night. There were no more dreams to make sense of. Yet she knew little of the Colonial House featured so prominently in her dreams. "What was Rachael trying to show her? Was she about to find out?"

Only the truth lay ahead of her now, but could it be more than she bargained for? There was only one way to find out. Face it. And face it she would have to today.

Catherine drew back the lace curtains in the bedroom. The sun was slowly rising, throwing the early morning light at the dressing table mirror on the far side of the room.

She glanced down to the street below. Sitting in the grey saloon car parked directly outside the house were the two FBI agents assigned to protect her and Izzy. This was an added security she had not initially wanted but now did not want dismissed, if at all. It made her feel safe. "The FBI agents must have gone and got themselves something to eat earlier," she thought. She could see they were drinking either tea or coffee out of takeaway cups and eating breakfast. Catherine squinted her eyes. She could vaguely make out a McDonalds recyclable brown carrier bag in the front seat of the car. This reminded Catherine of her own hunger. She had not eaten since mid-morning the previous day.

Putting on her dressing gown and slippers, she made her way downstairs to the kitchen. Izzy was still asleep. The house was quiet. The kettle purred to life breaking the silence of the kitchen. It was just beginning to get light outside. Catherine made herself a cup of tea.

She pulled up a chair and sat down at the wooden kitchen table. There was a packet of digestive biscuits in the cupboard above the sink, which she had distinctly remembered from the other day. She reached up and took several from the packet.

After finishing her tea, Catherine made her way upstairs, showered and washed her hair before Izzy woke up. She put on a pair of skinny jeans, and an orange V-neck sweater. She roughly dried her hair with the hair dryer before quickly using her heated ghd electric straighteners. Catherine had always thought her hair to be by far her best asset; long, dark, straight and thick with a slight kink to give it body.

Ready for the day, she made her way downstairs to the kitchen. The time was now 8 am. Catherine could hear Izzy moving about upstairs. She switched the Nespresso coffee machine on to make Izzy's morning Lungo coffee, and waited patiently for Izzy to come downstairs...

Chapter 55
2010

"Morning Catherine," Izzy spoke sleepily to Catherine. "Did you sleep well dear?" she asked, stifling a yawn.

"No not particularly Izzy," seeing as we were kidnapped yesterday, tied up, and all but shot at; not surprising really!!! And I met my father, whom I have waited all my life to meet, and found out he really is a bastard!!! Not one of my better days, Izzy?" Catherine scorned.

"Now, now dear, I know yesterday was a trifle hard, but we got through it with the help of Martin Castona and Brody, without them, I'm not sure what would have happened," Izzy replied, a trifle anxious at Catherine's response. Izzy was tough and well used to danger even for her mature years.

"Ok, I'm sorry I was a bit harsh, but I'm glad it's all over now and I won't have to meet Todd Clayton ever again," Catherine replied finalising the conversation and moving swiftly on.

Catherine poured Izzy a cup of coffee and handed it to her over the kitchen table. She sat down and waited for Izzy to let her into the dark secrets of her family's past as she had promised.

"OK dear, what I am about to tell you will come as a bit of a shock, but you are used to them now aren't you," Izzy said laughing, but trying to be serious. Your family's past was a lot darker than you originally envisaged and a lot more involved. Teddy and I tried to persuade Janet and Mike, your grandparents, not to go ahead with the plan, but they were adamant. They wanted to give their children and you, the kind of life that had eluded them, even though they worked hard all their lives. This was a chance of a lifetime for them. They had no intention of letting it slip by.

"Working for the CIA in the 70s and 80s was very unlike today," Izzy implied. "The pressure was much greater and the day to day implications on your life and sole were immense. There were no mobile phones, or internet – that was just surfacing, you had just your intuition to rely on. Sometimes Teddy and I would have liked to give it all up, but we were too involved; that would not have been a favourable choice, you were easily dispensable back in the day!!

"But I digress." Izzy sipped on her hot coffee. She began to reveal events leading to the present day.

"Well Janet and Mike had visited Todd Clayton's parents' home and accepted the sum of $2,000,000. This was on the understanding that Susie would have an abortion immediately and nothing would ever be heard of the matter again.

"But your grandparents had other ideas. They thought they could fool the Claytons. Have their grandchild, in secret, and disappear to the Cayman Islands, never to be seen again," Izzy continued. "And they nearly got away with it. Somehow Todd got wind of Susie giving birth, although she'd been sent away to her Aunt and Uncle's house in Canada in the countryside to have the baby, somehow he found out. The Claytons were furious. I remember how they tried everything in their power to find where the Krugers were and of course the money. I still believe the money was taken from government funds. Not personal funds of the Claytons."

"You were taken away to the Cayman Islands on holiday, and we followed shortly after. Rachael had always promised to watch out for Susie of which she did. And by all accounts, still is, if your dreams are anything to go by," Izzy stated sympathetically.

"They took such a chance. Did they not realise how ruthless the Claytons were? And that their lives would be in great danger from that point on Izzy?" Catherine said.

"Well, probably not to the extent we realise. I think the money paid a greater part in their thinking," Izzy denounced.

"The money was immediately placed in a bank account in the Cayman Islands. It was untraceable and never disclosed. As far as the IRS and other authorities were concerned, it didn't exist.

Janet confided in me that she had transferred an undisclosed amount to another account somewhere else, leaving a smaller amount in the Cayman Islands. I didn't know at the time where this other account was and Janet hoped it would never be discovered. This undisclosed account would then increase in value over the years, and would be purely for you Catherine. She did this for your future. The other account they hoped would never be traced back to the Cayman Islands and would help Susie and her baby, her brother and sister and Janet and Mike to start a new life. Unfortunately it was not destined to be," Izzy confided.

"The rest I think you know Catherine," Izzy continued. "We took charge of you, on our boat, whilst the Krugers transferred this separate amount to another account and another bank. It was on their return that the accident occurred. It was reported that there was a gas explosion on board their boat. They never made it back to the USA... Their bodies were never recovered, and the file was closed, after only a short time. This, as far as Teddy and I were concerned, smelt of corruption and danger. It must have been a cover up involving the authorities out there in the Cayman Islands, but we could never get to the bottom of it, without involving ourselves, and we had you to think of. Life went on and we returned to England with you," Izzy whispered, emotions getting the better of her.

"There is something else very important that I have to tell you," Izzy carried on... "Your father..."

The doorbell rang, momentarily lifting the heaviness in the air Catherine had felt for the last hour or so. "I'll go," said Izzy, "This will give you a little more time to digest what I have just told you dear."

Izzy walked out of the kitchen and into the hall to the front door. She could see the silhouette of Daniel Adams through the small glass window in the centre of the door. He was early but it was good to see him again. Izzy had always liked Daniel. She hoped Catherine felt the same way...

Chapter 56
2010

"Have you told her yet?" Daniel asked.

"No, I was just about to when you rang the doorbell," Izzy whispered. "Perhaps it would be best coming from you Daniel. She has to know the truth soon, and now is as good a time as any; she is expecting some sort of revelation, but probably not this Daniel. Be tactful and careful, don't manipulate the truth. Be honest with her."

"I will," Daniel replied. "I've waited for this day for a very long time. Well, here goes Izzy," he muttered tentatively under his breath.

He followed Izzy into the kitchen. Catherine was sitting waiting patiently now realising it was Daniel at the door, a bit early for their morning appointment.

"Morning Catherine," Daniel blurted out, before he had time to compose himself.

"Morning Daniel, it's nice to see you again, in slightly more informal surroundings," Catherine replied. "Would you like coffee or tea?"

"Ok thanks; that would be good. Coffee please, one sugar."

Daniel sat opposite Catherine at the kitchen table, whilst Izzy busied herself making Daniel's coffee.

"There is no easy way to tell you what I am about to reveal to you Catherine," Daniel stated nervously. "So I will get straight to the point. Todd Clayton, the man you know as your biological father, is in fact NOT your real father!" Daniel remained calm and carried on as best he could, his hands sweating, as anxiety took over. He composed himself, hesitating before speaking again. "The fact is Catherine, I AM your father," Daniel replied, instantly reaching out and taking Catherine's hands in his, to comfort her. "Yes I am your biological father."

"WHAT?" Catherine was lost for words. Her mouth had gone dry. Words were late in arriving. She tried to come to terms with the inconceivable news she had just been given. *Could my life be any more complicated?* "So, what you are telling me Daniel is that you are my REAL father? Rubbish, I don't believe you. My mother was raped by Todd Clayton, that's how she got herself pregnant. How on earth can you be my father? That's not the truth however much I would like it to be," Catherine replied angrily as she tried to make sense of what was being told to her.

"You will understand more when I have told you the 'full story,' "Daniel replied.

"Ok tell me," Catherine said, some of the anger momentarily leaving her, as she waited patiently for Daniel to explain.

Izzy handed Daniel a cup of coffee before he started his long awaited declaration.

"When I was at Yale University, there was a group of us. As friends we were inseparable. We hung about together, spent most evenings in the Blue Note Jazz Club, and were very close. Todd Clayton was one of those friends. He wasn't as bad a human being as he has achieved today, but still not to be trusted! For some reason your mother Susie was infatuated by him. As far as she was concerned, he could do no wrong. A week before the rape took place, we were all having a good night out in the Blue Note Club, and Susie was getting upset as usual during the evening, due to Todd flirting with anything that moved. He never did care about anyone, except himself, that was obvious from the start. That evening he disappeared with a local girl. He never returned.

"I remember Susie being so upset that night. She thought they were an item, her and Todd. Todd couldn't have been faithful to anyone if his life depended on it. She approached me. The tears were flowing freely down her face. I remember it well Catherine. I felt so sorry for her. At that time, Rachael and I hadn't started any sort of relationship, although I did have feelings for her, I must admit.

"Susie was inconsolable that night. I offered to take her back to the Dorm to make sure she got home safely. She accepted and we drove back to her Dorm. We were good friends Catherine, you have to understand that.

"Well one thing led to another. We made love. It just happened. I'm sorry to say Catherine. Although I did love Susie like a sister, there could never have been anything between us. It just would not have worked. But I think it helped Susie come to terms with Todd's behaviour. I like to think it gave her back herself worth. She was about to tell him, she wanted nothing more to do with him. I'm sure of that. Maybe he had fathomed that out for himself. We'll never know now. Apparently Susie wasn't sure who the father was, this I have only just found out. She told her parents the truth. I think Janet Kruger must have seen a way of making money out of a bad situation. The rest I know you are aware of Catherine."

Daniel sighed as he sat back in the wooden kitchen chair, thankful that the truth was now said.

"So I had my DNA tested against the blood that you give regularly at your local hospital. I had to pull a few strings to get the sample, but that is where a good friend of mine, John comes in very handy. It was 'positive'. That is how I know I AM your father Catherine. I hope I haven't disappointed you. I want you to know that you have gained a father who will always look after you, and I have gained a daughter that I thought I would never have," Daniel replied, relieved and grateful it was over now. All had been revealed – the truth had been told... or had it...?

Chapter 57
2010

Izzy asked Daniel to stay, if he didn't mind, and wait for Martin Castona to arrive.

Daniel sat quietly, listening to the soft chimes of the grandfather clock in the hall, and getting better acquainted with Catherine. There was so much of their past to catch up on. They knew it would take much longer than the time Daniel had to spare that day. He hoped it wouldn't be too long before they would see each other again, and continue where they left off.

The doorbell rang. "I'll go Catherine said, you sit and chat with Daniel." Catherine rose from her chair. Daniel reached across the kitchen table taking her hands in his. "I am so glad you are in my life Catherine, I hope we can have a great relationship together, I really do."

"I have a feeling we will Daniel," Catherine replied. "Yes, I'm pretty certain we will. "

Catherine walked out of the kitchen, down the hall and slowly approached the front door. Before opening the door to Martin, Catherine stood still in the hall. She felt a chill run down her spine. A warning she had come to rely on in the past; perhaps of an event that was about to unfold. It was never specific. She never could put her finger on. She wasn't sure what it was, but it was niggling at her. The doorbell rang again. Was it something she had overheard? Or could she sense something more sinister. She hoped whatever it was, it would be good news, and her instincts were on target.

Catherine had left Martin Castona standing outside the front door, for long enough. Unlatching the safety chain once more, she turned the brass latch and opened the heavy oak door. "Hello

Catherine, we meet again, but in far better circumstances this time, I'm pleased to say." Catherine looked at Martin, giving him a wry smile and a wink before closing the door behind him. She led him down the hall, and into the kitchen.

"Hello Martin, it's good to see you again," Daniel said, standing to greet him and reaching out to shake his hand.

"You too bud, it's been a while, eh?"

"You two know each other," Catherine stated in surprise?

"Well we've known each other a very long time Catherine," Martin replied; "in fact most of our lives." The silence surprised Catherine, as she slowly realised that on the face of it, it was a perfectly innocent statement. "But how do you know each other?" Catherine asked, rising slowly from her kitchen chair to face both Martin and Daniel.

Daniel hesitated before answering. He had no idea what Catherine's reaction would be. Was she ready for what was about to unfold before her? Daniel wasn't sure but there was no easy way to tell her. Here goes he thought to himself...

"Please sit down Catherine. There is something we all have to tell you. It will come as a shock to you, but I'm sure you are accustomed to a few shocks by now and it's the right time to reveal everything you should know about your family. You may have thought that you had no living relatives? But that is not true."

Catherine sat back down on the kitchen chair as Aunt Izzy took her hand in support.

"First of all it was not fate that brought you to Braeside School. This was engineered by Izzy with a little help from her connections. We were aware you were training to be a teacher, and the idea was to keep a watch on you, to keep you safe. We also understood Todd Clayton knew of your imminent inheritance and would stop at nothing to get his hands on it. This was our big chance to finally nail the bastard, even if you thought he was your father. It was a chance we had to take. I'm sorry Catherine but it was the only way to be sure," Daniel said.

Daniel glanced over at Martin. I would like to introduce you to your Uncle – Martin Castona. Of course this is an alias, and Martin is in fact, Travis Kruger, Susie's brother."

"What!!! Martin Castona – the Head at Braeside School, is my uncle?" Catherine sat completely bewildered. Her life falling apart, or was it now, at last, coming together. Travis rose from his seat and walked around the kitchen table. Putting his hands on Catherine's shoulders, he said. "I am so sorry Catherine, this will all be over soon and your life will return to normal, if somewhat drastically changed."

"There is someone else I will introduce to you at a later date. She is travelling over here as we speak. That is Natalie, my secretary. She is my sister and your Aunt Sarah. Yes, yet another bombshell for you to digest Catherine. She is very excited to meet you again, as part of our family, at long last. She does look somewhat different without her disguise, I will admit, so be prepared," Travis confirmed with a great deal of sympathy for Catherine.

Catherine sat, hands cupping her face, still unable to fully digest everything being thrown at her in the last few moments. "I have a family! I have a family!" Joy finally took over from despair.

Catherine looked over to Izzy, tears welling in her eyes. "I have a family Izzy, but Izzy you are my family and always will be, you know that don't you? You have always been there for me through thick and thin, I do love you Izzy."

Now it was Izzy's turn to get emotional. "You have been like a daughter to me, especially since my Teddy died. I love you too Catherine, very much." Daniel coughed nervously, breaking the emotionally charged atmosphere. "I'm sorry Catherine it's not quite over yet.

"This leads me to the next admission I have to make to you Catherine," Daniel replied.

"This will seem hard to comprehend at first but believe me it is true."

Catherine stared at both Izzy and Daniel. What was happening to her? It all seemed so surreal. What now? And more to the point, could there be anything else left for Daniel to reveal to her?

Daniel cleared his throat. He took Catherine's hands in his and slowly began…

Chapter 58
2010

"It's not much further now, Daniel explained, probably five miles at the most. They drove along the quiet suburban lane as Catherine glanced out of the car window. It was 'The Fall' – her favourite season. The leaves were still shadowing the trees with their beautiful hues of orange, red and green, some now falling as the soft breeze gently took them to the ground.

"Are you OK Catherine?" Daniel asked with concern. "Mmm. Yes sorry, just daydreaming."

"Well here we are ladies," Daniel confirmed as he drove into a parking bay of a large rambling house.

Catherine sat bewitched as she looked out of the car window, her eyes focusing on the old residential colonial house. This was the house she had seen on numerous occasions in her dreams. And here she was, actually outside. It stood proud in its grounds. Placed at the entrance to the house was a substantial hand painted plaque, delicately embellished in gold, its words gleaming in the early afternoon sunshine. "It's just how I remember it," Catherine thought to herself.

Izzy had a feeling this was the old colonial house that Catherine had often seen in her dreams and drawn as a child. The truth was now unfolding, which she had found almost impossible to keep from Catherine, but knew she had no choice. It would have been too dangerous to tell her.

"Try not to get upset dear, once we go inside the house Catherine," Izzy said. "It's going to be a great shock for you, but a nice one."

Daniel walked around the other side of the car and opened the rear door for Catherine. Stepping outside, she made her way quickly up the cobbled path, past the manicured lawns and flowerbeds, not waiting for anyone. She stood facing the hand-written board, which had eluded her for so long.

The plaque gleamed back at her in the bright sunshine – "Oakside Nursing Home."

"This house is a Nursing Home!" Catherine took several steps back, glaring at the plaque, in shock of what it at last had revealed to her. She moved slowly towards the steps that led up to the entrance of the house. The door was wide open. She could see inside. There were several uniformed nurses in blue and white, scurrying about their daily business.

Catherine didn't wait for Izzy, Daniel or Travis to catch up. She made her way up the steps and into the large foyer. The house's atmosphere was quiet and serene. A round mahogany table stood in the centre of the hall. Upon the table was a tall white and gold ornate vase. It held a large display of colourful country flowers, including lupines and hocks which Catherine remembered were growing in abundance at the entrance to the House. The perfume from the flowers as she passed the table was delicate and pleasing.

Catherine approached the foot of the stairs, and glanced upwards. Was it possible? She couldn't be sure, but she thought she caught a glimpse of a shadow moving up the hallway.

She couldn't remember reaching the top of the stairs. Her hands were clammy and shaking, and the hairs on her arms were standing on edge. There at the end of the corridor was a figure, still and motionless, but familiar to Catherine in many ways. Could it be, or was she imagining this? No this was real. The figure smiled and beckoned to Catherine to come forward.

Catherine felt as if she was rooted to the spot. But she knew she had to pass down the hallway towards the figure. As she drew ever closer, she was not wrong. Indeed it was Rachael. Standing directly in front of her, arms outstretched, welcoming her.

Catherine wanted so much to thank her for all the help she had given, bringing her to this point in her life, at last to know the truth. Without her this may not have been such a smooth transition.

Rachael beckoned to Catherine as she pointed to the door to room '201.' "Who is in this room? Please help me Rachael?" Rachael smiled once more and reached out to Catherine, whispering, "Goodbye Catherine and good luck" as she disappeared slowly down the corridor, slowly fading out of sight.

"No please come back, I want to thank you." But Catherine knew she would never see Rachael again. She had been there for her when she was needed, now it was up to her to forge her own future.

Catherine stood in front of the door with the brass plaque that read – 'Room 201.'

"There you are Catherine," Izzy puffed, as she tried to get her breath after climbing the flight of stairs too quickly. "I'm not as young as I used to be dear."

"How did you know which room to go to Catherine," Izzy questioned, but Izzy had a good idea by the expression on Catherine's face, and the fact that most of the colour had drained from it. "Are you OK dear? You look as if you've seen a ghost." Catherine turned and faced Izzy who had just regained her breath; "But I have Izzy, I have!" Izzy knew of Catherine's gift and accepted the fact that she had experienced something that only Catherine could explain and Izzy was sure she would later.

Before Izzy could answer, Daniel and Travis arrived. "Well here we all are Catherine," Daniel exclaimed. "We had better knock and go in…"

Chapter 59

Catherine stepped forward, knocking gently on the door of Room 201. She entered not waiting for a response. Travis, Daniel and Izzy followed directly behind her. It was a room of medium size, with two large windows on the far side. It felt warm and inviting as the sun streamed through the open windows bouncing off the crystal chimes hanging nearby.

The room was beautifully furnished with several pieces of antique furniture dominating the space. The bed with a painted wooden carved headboard was the focal point of the room. A small display cabinet stood on the far right of the room and a pink and green floral upholstered armchair was situated near the bed.

Looking around the room, Catherine could see several photographs in silver frames standing behind the glass of the display cabinet. They resembled that of family members and baby photographs, which were rather old, taken a long time ago.

Izzy took Catherine's hand. "Come Catherine I want you to meet someone." A figure sitting in a wheelchair directly in front of one of the open windows turned around very slowly sensing someone was approaching. "Hello Susie," Izzy whispered. "There is somebody here I want you to meet."

Catherine felt cold with the shock. Shivering in the warmth of the room, she moved forward as Susie looked up at her. Susie's hair was still a vibrant colour of the years past, but small glints of grey could be seen now, and her skin was still pale, smooth and translucent. Her beauty was undeniable, even as the years had progressed and taken their toll.

Tears were glistening in Susie's eyes as she spoke softly. "I knew you would come one day Catherine. I know it's you. I would know you anywhere. I have waited a long time for this moment," as she took Catherine's hand in hers and squeezed it tightly, not intending to let go. You are my baby daughter that I lost all those years ago. At last I have you back in my life Catherine where you belong. I knew Rachael would find you," Susie confirmed. The tears flowed freely down Susie's face, as tears welled in Catherine's eyes in disbelief. "Yes Catherine this is Susie Kruger, your mother," Izzy confirmed, as the sheer happiness of the moment overwhelmed them all.

Catherine had so many questions to ask her mother. They stayed in the room with Susie for an hour, chatting and getting better acquainted before the nurse entered the room, requesting they leave as it was Susie's rest period and time for meds.

They said goodbye and promised faithfully to return the following day to catch up fully, they left the room and Susie bid them farewell for the time being.

"What did Susie mean by, 'I knew Rachael would find you'?" Daniel asked Catherine puzzled by the statement, as they made their way down the curved staircase, and out into the chill of the late afternoon air. "I would tell you Daniel, but I fear you may not believe me." "Try me," Daniel replied anxious to know exactly what Susie meant.

"I will tell you later Daniel or should I say Dad," chuckling slightly out loud. "I'm still in shock. I just cannot believe what's happening to me. I need a good night's sleep, and I hope when I wake in the morning, it has not all been a dream," Catherine replied.

"Pinch me Daniel, so I know I'm not dreaming," Catherine asked as they walked down the pathway towards their waiting car.

Daniel waited several minutes before pinching Catherine on the arm. "Ouch!!! That was a bit severe," Catherine cried out. "I wanted to make sure you felt it," Daniel replied, getting his own back after the 'Dad' comment earlier. "Yes I felt it, thank you Daniel," giggling as they all walked on in the best of spirits.

Izzy knew she had a lot of explaining to do, but it would have to wait 'till later, until things had settled down and Catherine had come to terms with the outcome of the day. But would Catherine want to wait...?

Chapter 60

Catherine woke early the next morning, to a rather dull, drizzly overcast day, but this did nothing to dampen her spirits.

It was obvious no one wanted to talk the previous night on their return from the nursing home, so best things were left until the morning. Catherine was anxious to find out what had happened to her mother, Susie. Why was she in a wheelchair? How long had she been disabled? She must have survived the hit and run accident that happened years ago. Had she sustained major injuries to her back; had the nursing home been her permanent residence following her accident, and who was paying the cost of the home?

Daniel and Travis had slept the night at Izzy's. Travis slept on the sofa and Daniel on a 'put you up' in the spare bedroom. There was little point going home just to return the following day, so Izzy offered both Travis and Daniel a bed for the night, possibly not the comfort they were used to but for one night, acceptable.

"Good morning Travis," Catherine spoke, stifling a yawn. "Morning Catherine, you're up with the lark this morning," Travis replied, as he sipped a hot cup of freshly made coffee from Izzy's coffee machine. "Would you like a cup Catherine? Which is your favourite blend?"

"Yes please, great thanks Travis. That should wake me up, I'll have the Capriccio – not too strong," Catherine replied. Izzy always had a good supply of coffee pods for her machine she loved the blends of coffee they offered.

Daniel and Izzy were yet to surface. Catherine could hear movement upstairs, so it wouldn't be long before they made their way downstairs.

"Travis, please tell me what happened all those years ago," Catherine said, anxious to know. "Best wait for Izzy, she can fill in all the gaps and more," Travis said. "But there is something I want to talk to you about and something I would like to ask you. You can say no, or think about it and let me know in your own time," Travis replied.

Catherine looked puzzled as she slowly sipped her morning coffee. "Look I think I know you well enough now having spent a great deal of time at Braeside School with you over the last year and facing moments of danger recently together, I know that you could be of a great help to the Bureau with the gift that you possess," Travis hesitantly explained.

"It would be more of a consultancy position to start, where we would call upon you from time to time to help solve crimes beyond our realms," Travis confirmed. "Not that I can say I truly believe in the supernatural, but it seems there is a skill that you possess which could be of help to us at the Bureau, or should I say, for the unusual cases. I believe my sister Susie, your mother, has this gift, and again, like you, it never surfaced properly until she reached her 20s."

"What do you say Catherine?" Travis asked hopefully. "You could stay on at Braeside School as a teacher for the time being, but if things were to escalate it would be wise, if you so wished, to join us permanently on the staff, whenever you were required to help out. It would be nice to have you near, now that we are at last a family, and I can keep an 'eye on you,'" Travis smiled, hoping Catherine would be in agreement and see the funny side of his joke.

"Sarah and I will no longer be working at Braeside School. We were only there for one purpose and one purpose only, to keep you safe Catherine. Our objective has been completed and the Head of the School, James Stafford would continue his original role as agreed.

Catherine found it hard to hide her excitement. "Are you absolutely sure Travis? Has this gone through all the necessary channels before I give you my answer," Catherine almost shouted in excitement.

"Yes, it has been passed by my Head of Department" Travis now anxious for Catherine's answer.

"Well absolutely yes," was Catherine's answer, "yes, yes!!"

242

"But what if it doesn't work that way and I no longer have the gift, and I don't possess visions or dreams in the future to help with your investigations, what then Travis?"

"Well we will take one day at a time, but I am pretty sure you have this gift for life Catherine, as Susie confirms, she frequently has dreams and visions, like you, so I'm trusting you have the same ability. Susie is unable to help us fully because of her disability, but she is hoping you will step in and help whenever you can Catherine." Travis was visibly relaxed now knowing that Catherine had accepted his offer.

***

Izzy appeared at the kitchen door. She had on her usual pink dressing gown and fluffy slippers, often being held responsible for much 'mickey' taking by Catherine over the years. "Morning Izzy," Catherine said. "Your coffee is ready for you."

"OK thank you dear. Did you both sleep well?," Izzy questioned, helping herself to the mug of coffee freshly made, and sitting down at the kitchen table opposite Catherine and Travis.

"I know you want to know what happened to Susie after the accident Catherine, and you shall know the truth, as soon as Daniel is here. I think he is entitled to know exactly what happened, don't you," Izzy exclaimed.

Daniel came down the stairs and into the kitchen. He was fully dressed and washed, and wore a white polo shirt and jeans; he looked good and was everything Catherine could have ever have wished for in a father.

"Now you are all here I will tell you what happened on that fateful night, when both Rachael and Susie were walking back to their dormitory," Izzy said.

Daniel sat down on the remaining kitchen chair, as Izzy started to recall the event that took place many years ago .....

Chapter 61

"Do you believe in fate Daniel?" Catherine asked, knowing full well what the answer would be.

"No, no I don't, but after everything that has evolved over the last few months, I'm not sure what I believe anymore. I've never believed in delving into 'psychic surgery' of any kind, or things that 'go bump in the night', I feel these are well left alone," Daniel reiterated slightly sarcastically. "But to say you have dreamed things that have happened and seen visions, this I find hard to believe. I want so much for there to be just a glimpse of truth in what you tell me, but you don't have proof of any kind that would make me believe otherwise."

"If I tell you something Daniel, something that means nothing to me, but a great deal to the two people concerned, and you being one of them, do you think you may change your mind?" Catherine whispered.

A momentary silence could be felt around the kitchen table, as if time itself stood still. "What is it Catherine that you have to tell me?" Daniel remarked nervously. Travis and Izzy looked and listened with apprehension, neither aware of what was about to be revealed.

Catherine began to tell Daniel something that Rachael had spoken of in a past dream. It was a fleeting remark that meant little or nothing to Catherine at the time but now it seemed quite poignant that Daniel should know of it. She was hoping this might sway Daniel into believing there was some truth in what she had to say.

"The beach and Barbara Lewis," Catherine blurted out. "This message is what I believe Rachael wanted you to know Daniel, and that she would never forget that day. This has no meaning for me, but I think it does for you Daniel," Catherine insisted.

The colour could be seen slowly returning to Daniel's face, as he sat staring at the ring his coffee mug had made on the kitchen table in front of him. There was no denying Daniel was visibly moved, and Catherine thought she saw a glimpse of a tear leaving the corner of his eye. Was this an admission of belief or just Catherine's imagination?

"Well I think we can safely say, can we, this means quite a lot to you Daniel?" Catherine asked.

Daniel chose his words carefully. "Yes a great deal Catherine," he replied. He began to relay what had happened on that day at the beach. "It was the last time that Rachael and I were together before that fateful accident. It is etched in my memory forever...

"We headed to the beach for the day. Rachael looked beautiful. I remember the breeze lifting her long dark hair away from her face as it rested on the slightly tanned skin of her bare shoulders. We had a lot of fun that day." Daniel spoke softly and said; it was the day I fell in love with Rachael, that day at the beach.

"The day passed all too quick. We lay on the beach, looking up at the dark blue evening sky and the lights surrounding the beach house. "It was a Barbara Lewis record, 'Baby I'm Yours' that could be heard playing softly in the background, drifting out from the juke box inside the beach house. **I will never forget that day as long as I live.**"

"Now will you believe me Daniel," Catherine pleaded.

"I guess I want to. You couldn't possibly have known about that day. We promised each other not to say a word to anyone, as our relationship had only just started. You know what people are like. It would have been all around campus before we knew it. That was our vow to each other, so I know Rachael would not have told a soul, not even Susie," Daniel said now visibly moved. "And I certainly didn't! Wow!! How can I come to terms with this?" Daniel questioned, rising from the kitchen chair to get another cup of coffee.

Travis and Izzy looked at each other almost in disbelief. Had Catherine revealed something so prevalent as to bring Daniel to a state of shock?

Travis broke the atmosphere with a well-deserved overdue statement. "You will all be pleased to know that our friend Todd Clayton has admitted, possibly under duress I believe, to the 'hit and run' accident involving Susie and Rachael 20-odd years ago. He also wants eight other crimes to be taken into account at his trial. I wouldn't be at all surprised if he has something up his sleeve. Why would he plead guilty to all those crimes, knowing full well what the outcome would be, if there was not something in it for him? Or, more likely, his father is involved somewhere down the line. "I wouldn't put it past that bastard!!"

***

"Changing the subject, I expect you are looking forward to your 'windfall' Catherine," Daniel asked, "now that everything is falling into place? The amount you receive will depend on the 'finder's fee' and what you are able to keep from the initial investment. This will take several weeks if not a little longer to sort out, but worth the wait I expect you'll agree."

Catherine had no intention of holding on to all the money she would get. A certain amount would stay in an investment account for her future, but the remainder would be shared between her Aunt Izzy, Travis, Sarah, Susie and of course Daniel for all their help in bringing Todd Clayton to justice but more importantly, knowing she has her biological mother in her life. But who had been paying the bill for Susie at the Nursing Home, for all those years...?

"Izzy can you tell me who...

Knock!! Knock!! The sound of the front door knocker echoed loudly in the hall. "I wonder who that can be" Izzy questioned? "It's more than likely it's the postman he never delivers at the same time more than once a week!"

"I won't be a moment Catherine." I'll see if the postman has a delivery for me, or it may well be for a neighbour, then we can all have a good breakfast, maybe I'll make some blueberry pancakes, before we visit Susie this afternoon. I know how much you like them dear." Izzy had only just recently been informed that Susie was in fact alive and she was so excited to be part of Catherine's reunion with her mother, and to see Susie again.

Izzy rose from the kitchen table, mug in hand, to answer the front door. Catherine, Travis and Daniel were much more relaxed in each

247

other's company, chatting and fully aware that the trauma was over and life would now resume some sort of order...

"CRASH!!"

"What was that?" Catherine cried out. Travis, Daniel and Catherine all stood up quickly from the kitchen table. Running down the hall towards Izzy, they could see the pieces of the smashed coffee mug scattered around on the hall floor. Izzy was pale and shaking, staring at the open front door.

"Hello Catherine! We have waited a very, very long time for this day, and to finally meet you. We had better formerly introduce ourselves hadn't we?"

"We are Janet and Mike Kruger, your grandparents"

----- THE END -----

.

Lightning Source UK Ltd.
Milton Keynes UK
UKHW01f1803110618
324082UK00001B/51/P